Once Again

ONCE AGAIN

GINA L. SCOTT

Golden Star Publishing

This is a work of fiction. Names, characters, events, and places are used fictitiously or are a product of the author's imagination. Any resemblance relating to persons living or dead, events or locations portrayed in this novel are entirely coincidental.

To order copies of "Once Again" please visit www.goldenstarpublishing.com

For

My amazing husband Doug and my wonderful kids –
Sherilyn, Arianne, and Zack.

Your encouragement and support allowed my dream
to come true.

PROLOGUE

She had that same dream again last night and wondered why she couldn't dissect it like she had been able to do with all her other dreams. She knew *exactly* where she had been in her dream. She was in a tunnel – and she was running. But, from what? And why? She always seemed to wake up at the exact moment their eyes met. And, although she didn't know whom those eyes belonged to, they somehow felt good and made her smile. Yes, she always woke up with a smile when she had that dream.

CHAPTER ONE

It was a chilly morning in Lancaster, Pennsylvania and, as usual, Savannah was running late. Why had she stayed out so late again last night? She had known she would pay for it this morning but Trish, her friend since kindergarten, had begged her to stay at the crowded club just a little longer. She and Bill were arguing again and Trish had wanted her there for moral support. Not that she was any help. They went off in a corner and left her sitting at a table, alone, listening to the band.

The place was small for the large crowd in attendance. Booths lined the outer sidewalls and small tables were scattered around the dance floor. The band was set up in the back of the room allowing the most optimum space for dancing and listening to music. The group was pretty good and Savannah enjoyed hearing the cover songs of the past. It had only been 10 years since high school graduation, but it seemed like a lifetime and already the songs of that time period seemed old and nostalgic. She looked at her watch, then glanced at her friend sobbing quietly with her arms around her boyfriend, and knew it was finally time to go. Savannah stood up knowing that the tears were probably happy tears but she wasn't completely convinced. She sauntered a little closer to try to get within earshot and get a better view and accidently bumped in to a very drunk woman. Actually the inebriated woman bumped into Savannah and started screaming. The yelling was awful. What a scene she was causing and it was all directed at Savannah!

Savannah looked around for a fast exit knowing full well that there would be no reasoning with the belligerent lady and felt that putting space between them rapidly would end the drama that was quickly brewing.

The band started playing a slow song that diverted everyone away from the situation and on to the dance floor. As the crowded room of singles began to pair up, the space became a mix of slow moving bodies gently rocking to and fro in the dim light.

Savannah felt a nudge on her elbow and, as she turned, saw a man smiling down at her asking her if she would like to dance. Before she had time to think about it or respond at all, he had whisked her in to the middle of the swaying bodies leaving her no other option but to dance. She was a little flustered and for a moment, just listened to the music and took everything in. He smelled incredible – clean and manly. She noticed *that* right away. He definitely knew how to dance and swept her around the room as if they were the only ones in it. She looked up to find him smiling down at her and couldn't help but notice the aura of something so powerful that it pulled her to him like a magnet. The connection was something she had never experienced before and the intense feeling was surging through her entire body as if she were being shocked. Smiling back with flushed cheeks she wondered if he could tell how she felt and, more importantly, if he felt it too.

Just then, Trish came rushing over to her, grabbed her arm and dragged her away before she could even thank the sweet smelling man for the dance. Looking at Trish, Savannah suddenly realized that the tears she had witnessed earlier had not been happy tears as they continued to stream down her face even now, creating a black trail of mascara as they traveled. Her long blonde hair that had been in a tightly wrapped bun was down now, around her face, and her blue eyes were already swelling from the constant flow of tears.

Outside in the brisk evening air, Trish caught her breath and told Savannah it was over. The look on her face was crushing and Savannah hugged her knowing full well the pain of a broken relationship and not envying the long laborious road of recovery Trish had in store for her. They went down to the corner and had a cup of coffee and Savannah listened to every detail of the horrible break up.

It was 2:30 a.m. before she finally opened the door to her apartment and literally dropped into bed. The last thing she thought about before she went to sleep was how bad she felt for her best friend. She remembered the pain from her past like it was yesterday. But, it had been over two years ago, and she had vowed to never let a man in her life again. She would work hard and become the head of a company and she would volunteer to help wherever needed, but she would never let another man hurt her as Joel had done. She was determined to make better choices in her life now, than she had made in the past, and felt confident that she was on the right path to success. Savannah would have to rehash those feelings again but would do it to give Trish the strength she needed. She would be strong enough for both of them.

CHAPTER TWO

Work was busy, as usual, but Savannah loved it. She was in the sales and marketing department for a small start up company that was getting ready to launch an innovative product. Being in the forefront for new products was exhilarating and filled her life with excitement at every turn. She had met so many people, all with fascinating backgrounds and abounding energy. She loved the collaboration between the staffing levels and departments and loved the way all ideas were welcomed, reviewed, and either refined or recycled. The company motto for suggestions was:

Reveal

Review

Refine/Recycle

Every idea was looked at and all members of the staff were able to contribute in a safe environment. The small group of fewer than 50 people knew that if, and when, the company sold the product, each employee would be wealthier than their wildest dreams. But until then, there was work to be done and being tired didn't help. Savannah had made a note to herself not to go out again during the week.

Over the last month, Savannah's group had been busy with the final phase of their signature product. It was a special tool that would allow the consumer to double their production time when processing any kind of fruit or vegetable by peeling, squeezing, chopping, dicing or pureeing it in record time. Although the original prototype was for commercial use, a smaller home-based model could be on the market soon after the initial commercial release, if all went well. From there, the possibilities were endless. Savannah's team had shared some really good ideas and now it was her job to fly to California to meet with a manufacturing company to see if they would make the prototype. The hope was that they would be interested in the product and want to invest in it after the model was made. Her boss, Ted, had done some research and felt that the company she was going to meet with, *The Ripe and Ready Fruit Company,* would be able to make the product with ease. Because they were also in the business of selling fruits and vegetables, Ted knew that they would be the most likely investor for the tool. It was Savannah's job to pitch the product to them.

She was looking forward to her trip as she had only been to California once, when she was little, and unbeknownst to her, had unreasonable weather expectations of the west coast. Even though it was October, she was looking forward to lying out on the warm sunny beach after her presentation and had allowed herself a few extra days in order to do so.

As she was deciding what to pack, she called Trish to see if maybe she could sneak away and come with her. She figured the trip away would do her good, and because Savannah hadn't had a lot of time to really talk to her since the break up, she was feeling guilty and thought the trip would be really good "girl time."

Trish picked up the phone on the first ring and Savannah was surprised at the cheerfulness in her voice. After talking for a few minutes, Savannah invited her to visit the west coast with her. Trish accepted the invitation with excitement in her voice and by the time they got off the phone, they had made plans to meet at their favorite coffee shop the next morning, to tie up last minute details. They would leave a week from Wednesday, with plans to return home late Sunday afternoon. Savannah's presentation was scheduled for first thing Thursday morning and they would have the rest of that day and the weekend to do whatever they wanted in sunny California.

The week before the trip was filled with numerous meetings and late night working sessions to put finishing touches on the presentation, but Savannah managed to get away one evening to shop for some "west coast" clothes. After buying shorts, sundresses, high heels, and wedge sandals she found two flattering bathing suits that she picked up on clearance. She was sure that California was going to be a tropical paradise and couldn't wait to get there.

At the end of the shopping spree she felt pleased with her purchases and was amazed that she liked how she looked in the clothes she had bought. *It must be my state of mind*, she thought as she hailed a taxi to go home. The cab was warm and smelled like cinnamon. She smiled as she looked out the window daydreaming about her upcoming trip and watching the leaves blow by her as the cool October wind started to pick up.

Wednesday arrived with a blistering chill that soon gave way to an icy rain. *Great*, she thought. *I am going to be in the air with this horrible storm. But, I'm going to California.* Somehow that thought made everything all better.

Savannah rushed out the door after checking to make sure she had everything for her trip. Her cell phone rang and startled her. Glancing at the caller ID she saw Trish's smiling face looking back at her. She picked up the phone and locked the door behind her moving quickly down the stairs to the waiting cab. She realized that she had been so busy that she hadn't touched base with Trish to decide on a meeting place at the airport and was glad that Trish had taken the initiative to call her. Savannah was out of breath as she heard Trish say that she would not be able to go to California with her. She had reconnected with her boyfriend Bill and he had proposed! In all the excitement she had forgotten about the trip until late last night and hadn't wanted to leave a message.

Savannah was in shock. She was happy, sad, and excited all at the same time. She had a million questions for her but no time to ask them as she had a plane to catch. Trish explained that she had already given up her ticket and, since it was a full plane, some lucky person on standby would now get to go.

The cab ride to the airport was treacherous given the hazardous road conditions. It always amazed Savannah that the cab drivers didn't slow down one bit and managed to get passengers to their destinations. Today was no exception and because she had been on a roller coaster of a taxi ride, she hadn't had time to think of anything but getting to the airport in one piece.

After going through the security line and checking in her suitcase, she walked over to get a caramel mocha coffee drink and relax. She hadn't realized how badly her nerves were shot until she took a moment to sit.

The realization that she was going to California alone came skidding to the forefront of her mind like a car out of control. She straightened up quickly and spilled her hot drink on her beautiful new white jacket. Frustrated and nervous, she got up to go to the restroom to see if she could salvage the coat and get the mocha out before it stained. She glanced at the clock and noticed she had about 10 minutes before boarding. *Well*, she thought, *so much for being able to relax.*

She wasn't a good flyer and had really been looking for the support and distraction that Trish would have provided during the five-hour flight. *Things to be thankful for*, she thought. *It has stopped raining – at least for now.*

She was the very last one to board the plane and she was thankful that she had paid extra to have an assigned seat. Otherwise, she would have been seated at the worst part of the plane probably next to a cranky baby or an overweight snoring old man. The flight attendant helped her put her carry-on luggage up in the rack since they were ready to go and it seemed that everyone was waiting for her. She saw the last window seat and made a beeline to get there quickly.

As she approached her row she glanced at her fellow isle passengers and realized that the man sitting in the middle seat, where Trish was suppose to have been sitting, was the man who had asked her to dance a month earlier at the club.

A burning glow covered her face as she excused herself to move in and settle in to her window seat. The isle passenger was already nodding off and seemed annoyed at the inconvenience, but the man in the middle smiled and stood up to give her more room. As she squeezed by, she could smell the captivating scent of the man that had swept her off her feet. It instantly brought her back to that evening and how she felt with him looking down at her smiling. She sat down and looked out the window, face still burning with embarrassment. Or was it something else?

She wondered why she was so flustered and thought back if Joel had ever made her feel this way. These seemed to be new feel-ings, ones she wasn't sure *what* to do with and ones she wasn't sure she *wanted* to deal with.

The plane was up in the air in moments and she was glad she hadn't had time to overreact to the take off. She would have embarrassed herself in front of the handsome stranger who seemed to keep reappearing in her life.

After they had been flying awhile, the seat belt light went off and everyone seemed a little more at ease. The cabin was filling with a small lull of voices when Savannah's seat companion leaned over to tell her that she looked familiar. He wanted to know if they had met before.

The nerve, she thought. Apparently she hadn't done to him what he had done to her. She was furious and told him that she hadn't thought they had met and quickly turned her head and leaned over to look out the window. He straightened up and leaned back but not before leaning in first, which allowed her to experience that powerful aroma that left her dizzy. She wasn't sure if it was some magical cologne or what exactly it was but it was doing a number on her and she felt her cheeks burning again. When the flight attendant came to take their drink order it was all she could do to blurt out what she wanted without sounding like a fool. She thought she noticed a little smirk on the side of his mouth. She was dumbfounded. What was going on? What was he doing to her? Not only had she not experienced these feelings before, she had vowed to never even *think* of another man again. Now, he had her flustered and uncomfortable and she hadn't said more than two words to him!

The flight attendant handed her the drink she had ordered and Savannah declined any other food service for the remainder of the trip. She had decided that her next meal was going to be in California and she couldn't wait.

She closed her eyes to think about all the things she was going to do. She also thought a little more about her presentation and what she was going to say. She thought it strange that the man sitting next to her could completely tear down the confident façade that she wore all the time. She held a high level position with the company she worked for and was quite the seasoned public speaker. That is why she had been chosen to pitch the idea and get the prototype made. It was also why she was so surprised at how tongue-tied she seemed to be next to this stranger.

She wished she could get up and sit somewhere else. Sitting between a crying baby *and* an overweight snoring old man now seemed much more appealing than sitting so close to this man that was making her very uncomfortable with his arrogant attitude and bewitching effect. Every time she shifted away he seemed to shift a little closer making the small space between them shrink a little more with every move. Her neck had a kink in it from straining to look out the window and she was getting ready to just turn around and say something to him when he tapped her on the shoulder and asked if she would like a pillow. Apparently, the flight attendant had tried to get her attention and she had been so lost in her own thoughts that she hadn't heard the question. He smiled as he handed her the pillow as if he had run to the store to pick it out himself. She opened her mouth to say something but he turned abruptly and starting chatting with the flight attendant, who was giggling like a young schoolgirl. That made Savannah even *more* furious. They went back and forth with their flirtatious comments and Savannah wished she had bought the headphones that she had seen in one of the little souvenir shops she had passed in the airport. As the flight attendant finally went on her way, the captivating stranger sitting next to her inched closer again. She made a decision that she wasn't going to push away and wanted to see who would win the battle of personal space. She thought, *I wonder if he thinks he can just pour on his charm and get whatever he wants. Well*, she thought, *he will lose this war because I am not going to fall under his spell.*

The five-hour flight dragged and she hadn't said one word to her flying buddy. She thought that strange as he had been so flirtatious with the flight attendant but had made no attempt to talk to her whatsoever. The pilot's husky voice finally came over the speaker saying they were getting ready to make their decent to Santa Barbara. He reported that the weather was warm and sunny, a balmy 82 degrees with a slight warm breeze. *Perfect*, she thought and a chill went through her as she remembered the cold rainy weather she had left several hours earlier in Lancaster. She was excited about being in California and knew that she needed to seal the deal on this prototype and get her company's product into production. She was thrilled about the turn her life was about to take and was very ready for whatever opportunities lied ahead. What she wasn't ready for was for what happened next.

The landing was smooth and before she knew it, passengers were debarking from the plane rather quickly. The man on the isle seat had a problem retrieving his carry-on bag from the overhead bin. After wrestling with it for a few minutes, he was finally able to release it from its tight quarters and at last headed down the isle. The stranger next to her had been standing, waiting patiently, and Savannah had been given a chance to steal a good look at him without him noticing. He was about six feet tall, but seemed much taller compared to her 5' 5" frame. He had an average build and had dark hair and twinkling hazel eyes. He had a killer smile that could melt an iceberg and he seemed to have everyone he came in contact with under his charming spell. She caught her breath when he suddenly turned and looked straight at her. Their eyes met and locked and Savannah turned away quickly so that he wouldn't see her once again flushed face. She grabbed her bag and started down the narrow isle wondering what the issue was that left her so completely unarmed when it came to this man. She didn't even know his name. In fact, she knew nothing about him other than he had been at a club in Lancaster a month ago, he smelled amazing, and had some kind of magical pull on her that was driving her crazy. As he descended out of site through the walkway, she felt a sense of relief. She needed all her wits about her as she was far away from home, alone in a strange city, and had an important meeting in less than 24 hours that she had to be ready for. A lot was riding on this meeting and she was going to give it everything she had.

Savannah turned the corner to exit the plane and the tip of her heel lodged itself in a small hole between the plane door and the jet bridge, which knocked her off her feet. She landed, abruptly, on the walkway with her heel still caught and her foot still partly in her shoe. As she tried to get up, she squealed with the pain that shot up through her leg. She looked down and noticed her ankle swelling at a remarkable speed.

One attendant rushed to get ice while another helped guide the rest of the passengers around Savannah and off the plane. Savannah sat helplessly facing the plane door and thinking about what her next move was and a sense of panic came over her. The flight attendant, the one that had been flirting with the man in the seat next to her, asked if she was meeting someone that could help her get to a doctor. Before Savannah could say anything, the man that had been her nemesis on the plane was standing next to her saying that he would help her get to where she needed to be. The flight attendant looked almost hurt as she acknowledged what he said and walked away.

They were staring at each other once again. Savannah looked into his eyes and now noticed a gentle kindness behind that twinkle. She was scared and didn't know what to do. He looked at her, smiled, and said, "I don't think we have been properly introduced. My name is Jim." Savannah crumbled.

CHAPTER THREE

The ride to the urgent care facility was silent. It hadn't helped that once Savannah had regained her composure, she took on a defensive attitude asking to see his credentials. She wanted to find out exactly who he was and made sure that airline staff had the information as well. They were to notify her boss Ted, and let him know what had happened and that a gentleman named "Jim" was taking her to urgent care. Although all pertinent information regarding this man was hers for review, she wasn't able to read any of it. She was so shaken up that once she saw his driver's license picture, she got distracted and had to look away. Airline staff had assured her that they had all the critical information on both of them and gave them directions to the nearest urgent care facility. She felt a little safer knowing that someone would know what happened to her if he wasn't trustworthy and hoped that the airline staff would follow up, as they had said they would, to make sure she arrived at the medical office safely.

Now, with safety details behind them, the unnerving magnetic pull was busy at work. She tried to ignore the fact that it was one sided since he couldn't quite *put a finger* on if and when they had met before. With all the hoopla going on at the airport, she had only managed to hear that his name was Jim and he was in California on a business trip. The irony was uncanny.

The urgent care office was crowded. Jim sat down next to Savannah and handed her the paperwork to complete. She filled out the documents and handed them back to him a little reluctant that he now had the opportunity to see her home address and a lot of other personal information. She had no choice however, because her ankle was very swollen and seemed to be getting worse by the minute. She had leaned on him pretty heavily as they had made their way up the ramp and she was dizzy with the captivating aura he seemed to give off.

In a feeble attempt to break the silence, she looked over at him and tried to think of something to say. Her eyes met his and she realized that he had been staring at her for some time. Her face turned an autumn shade and she looked down. A quick recap of the last few hours' events flooded her head and persuaded her to return his gaze, as she knew she was stuck. He smiled that charismatic smile that melted her heart.

"Thank you for taking me here" she managed to say. "You don't have to wait. It looks like it is going to be awhile. I can take a cab to the hotel when I am done. I will be fine."

She so wished Trish had been there as she didn't feel *fine* at all. Her ankle hurt, she was in a strange place, and she was more than a little nervous about how she was going to get around in this unfamiliar city. But she wasn't about to show that vulnerable side right now.

Jim chuckled and said, "I don't have anything else that I need to be doing right now and besides, you are going to need help getting your stuff to the hotel. It just so happens we are staying at the same place. When you had us both give our life history to the airline staff, I heard the name of your hotel. I happen to be staying there as well so this will work out just fine." Savannah was exasperated. She was helpless and couldn't seem to get away from this guy. Just then the nurse called her name.

An hour and a half later she had a tight bandage on her ankle and crutches under her arms. A grade one sprained ankle was the diagnosis and she was advised to stay off it as much as possible. It would take five to fourteen days to heal.

Jim carried her belongings while she hobbled alongside him. She was thankful that she had packed a pair of flats in her bag just in case her feet got sore from the high heels she had been wearing. She made a mental note to throw those heels away as soon as she got home.

The hotel was beautiful, just like the picture on line, and she was happy that they had finally arrived. Check-in was smooth and the staff offered to wheel her to her room with their loaner wheel chair. She took them up on their offer anxious to finally have the opportunity to put some space between her and Jim. She wasn't sure why she felt the need to be away from him. She thought it could have been because she was so drawn to him and she didn't like it. She felt very vulnerable.

Distance will make me stronger, she thought and with that again thanked him and was on her way.

Once in her room she set out to make arrangements to get to her meeting the next morning. She knew her ankle would still be swollen and she wouldn't be able to get around easily. She arranged to have a cab pick her up and get her to her meeting and then return her to the hotel.

Well, she thought, *I might not be able to go shopping and see the sights but I will be able to enjoy the beautiful hotel and lounge by the pool.* She glanced out the window and noticed the sun was already making its decent. She thought about hobbling down to the restaurant she had noticed earlier when the hotel assistant had wheeled her through the lobby but upon trying to stand, realized that there was no way she would be able to get down there easily. She opted for room service instead and decided she would spend a relaxing night eating dinner in her room. She hopped over to the glass slider and opened it for some fresh air. She could hear the faint sound of waves clapping the shore in the distance and felt happy in spite of her swollen ankle.

She reviewed her notes for the upcoming meeting and learned that *The Ripe and Ready Fruit Company* that she was hoping would invest in the fruit and vegetable cutting prototype, was nationally known with offices sprinkled throughout several states. Noting all the locations she found it strange that her boss sent her to California, all the way on the west coast, when there was a plant right there in Lancaster. *I must be visiting headquarters*, she decided, and felt honored that he had chosen her for this very important task.

At 6:30 p.m. she closed the notebook she had been reviewing as she felt that she had done enough work for the day. She called for room service and ordered a bowl of clam chowder soup and a candied nut gorgonzola salad. She ordered a glass of red zinfandel, her favorite, and had decided to eat her dinner out on the balcony. The air was warm for October, nothing like she routinely experienced in Lancaster, and she was happy to be here, swollen ankle and all.

She changed into some black yoga pants and a purple T-shirt and settled down to wait for her meal. Within minutes, there was a knock on the door. The hotel assistant had mentioned that the hotel services were second to none but she was quite surprised by their efficiency as she heard the knock. She had planned to move closer to the door to be ready but hadn't anticipated such prompt service and it took her a moment to grab a crutch.

"Just a minute," she called out as she hopped on one crutch over to the door. A bead of sweat dripped down her face as she turned the door handle and opened the door wide to accept her meal that she assumed would be wheeled in on a cart. But, instead of the room service attendant she was once again staring straight at Jim.

Oh my God, she thought. She wiped the dripping sweat from her forehead and just stood there too mortified to do anything else. It had taken every last bit of energy to get to the door quickly and she knew she was completely disheveled. He on the other hand, looked like he was ready for a night on the town. He was wearing dark grey jeans that fit just right and a forest green button down shirt that brought out a green tint in his hazel eyes. The sleeves were rolled up halfway for a more casual look. His hair was tousled a little and his 5:00 shadow was making its debut. He smiled that amazing smile which made her knees start to buckle and her insides churn with unfamiliar desire.

He had a bottle of wine and two glasses in his hand. "I thought you might like some company," he said.

"How did you"....and then she stopped. He must have been right behind her when the assistant was getting the information about her room number and location. Was she destined to get to know him? She thought about it for a second – she was a big believer in destiny. She then hopped aside allowing room for him to come in. She couldn't believe that she was letting a perfect stranger in to her room. What was wrong with her? She closed the door as she watched him walk right through the room and on to the balcony. He set the bottle and two glasses down and looked up at her. As she started to limp over, there was another knock on the door. Her dinner had arrived but somehow she was no longer hungry. It amazed her that she hadn't eaten since breakfast but couldn't imagine eating anything right now. Her mind was wandering. *This is crazy*, she thought. She asked the attendant to set her food on the table in the room. Jim motioned for him to bring it outside, tipped him and sent him on his way. *It is going to be an interesting evening*, she thought and smiled.

Jim had already eaten but opened the wine. Noticing the glass of wine on her tray, he picked it up and handed it to her after she had carefully seated herself in one of the balcony chairs. With wine glasses in hand they sat quietly and looked at the stars that were gathering for the evening. The breeze was warm and slowly sailed by making the moment flawless. After a few sips of wine she realized that she was starving and had better eat. The clam chowder was the best she had ever had and, without thinking, she offered to share it with Jim. He leaned over for a bite and she found herself spoon-feeding him. The closeness of him stirred those feelings up once again and she sat up and leaned away. He smiled and looked away as well.

The waves rushing to shore stole the silence from the moment and soon they started talking. As it turned out, Jim worked for the company that Savannah was going to be meeting with in the morning. He was in charge of overseeing "new projects" the company might be working on and investing in. They laughed at how many coincidences had occurred and started talking business beginning with the meeting scheduled in the morning.

In business mode Savannah was stellar and the nervousness and awkwardness gave way to a strong confident woman. Jim was impressed with the way she presented her project and with the way she had thought of every angle. Jim had asked her again if they had met before the plane ride and now she felt comfortable enough to tell him that they had danced once, a month ago, in a nightclub back in Lancaster. Jim laughed at the memory.

"I *knew* you looked familiar. It was so dark in there and you were gone before I even had a chance to ask your name. Still, there was something about you that I didn't forget. I went looking for you a little later but you were gone."

They laughed and talked a little more about the band that had been playing that night and the song they had danced to, one of the famous love songs from 1975.

The wine was gone and it was getting late. They agreed that they had better call it a night, as they knew they both had an early morning meeting. Although Jim offered to drive her, Savannah declined as she had already made other arrangements and it was too late to change them.

She thanked him for the wine and coming over to keep her

company. This time when he left, she didn't feel embarrassed or frustrated. She felt something else...

CHAPTER FOUR

The alarm went off all too soon and as Savannah went to get up she winced at the throbbing pain. She pulled the covers back to reveal a swollen black and blue ankle and wondered how she was ever going to make it to the meeting, or even make it down to the lobby. She took a deep breath and threw her legs over the side of the bed. She kept reminding herself that she still had one good ankle and she could hop around on one foot just fine.

Although it took her twice as long to get ready, she had allowed herself that extra time and was right on schedule. She arrived at the elevator just as the doors were opening and slowly hopped in. Jim had helped her put some towels around the ends of the crutches the night before which helped protect her already sore armpits and she could feel the benefit the extra padding provided. She had straightened her dark hair and pulled it up on the sides but left her bangs to swing to the side of her forehead. She wore black slacks with a peach colored blouse and a black blazer. She was thankful that she had black flats to wear instead of the wedged sandals she had originally planned for the outfit.

The cab pulled up to a tall glass building, nestled between several other beautifully architected office buildings, and the driver actually got out of the car to help Savannah out. *Californians are really nice*, she thought, and gave him a large tip. She was going to the 3rd floor and, for the first time since she started her California adventure, she had butterflies in her stomach. She looked at the sign in front of the building that boldly stated "*The Ripe and Ready Fruit Company*." Savannah smiled and adrenaline rushed through her entire body.

She made her way slowly through the glass doors, careful not to irritate her sore arms any further. Reading the floor descriptions she discovered that manufacturing and development occupied the first floor and the next level housed the general offices, copy room and mailroom. The third floor description read "Mahogany Square." She pressed the button with the big number 3 on it since that was the floor she had been told to go to for the presentation. During the elevator ride, she wondered why the floor had been given that name. Her question was answered as the metal doors parted. She was greeted by a large mahogany workstation that encompassed the entire entryway to the floor. A woman in her mid 30s sat behind the desk and greeted Savannah with a smile.

As Savannah hobbled up to the desk she realized that she had only minutes to spare. The receptionist ushered her passed several offices, each with a mahogany door, before stopping at the large mahogany double-doors that opened to a rather large conference room. Although the entire floor wasn't big, the conference room was located at the opposite end from the elevator and it had taken Savannah a few extra minutes to get there. Upon entering the room, Savannah looked around and noticed there were about 20 people already seated. All eyes looked at the door as she made her way over to the nearest empty chair and sat down. There was a lot riding on this deal. Everyone from her company was counting on her to pitch this idea and get them to make this prototype and she was not about to let them down.

Savannah scanned the room looking for any sign of Jim but he wasn't there. She wondered if he had overslept or if something had happened to him. *Maybe he is in charge of a different new project,* Savannah thought. Well, the meeting was just about to start and she would have to think about him later.

A middle-aged woman stood up and introduced herself as the Project Manager for new development. Savannah recalled that her boss had told her that a seasoned project manager was going to be heading up the meeting and that she had been with the company for quite a few years.

Carlie, as she called herself, seemed like she had done her homework and was ready to listen to Savannah's pitch. She was leading the meeting and after introducing Savannah to the group, asked what had happened to put her on crutches. Savannah gave a quick replay of what had occurred and quickly changed the subject back to the matter at hand. She thanked them for allowing her to give her presentation and let them know how much she appreciated the opportunity to be there. Carlie asked everyone to go around the room and introduce themselves to Savannah.

The introductions were just about over and Savannah was getting ready to stand up and start her presentation. She had brought her laptop and had noticed that she only had to plug it in to have the slideshow she had prepared appear on the overhead screen at the front of the room. Just then, the receptionist that had guided Savannah to the conference room popped her head in and whispered something in Carlie's ear. Carlie nodded and said, "Our CEO is in town and would like to be in on the presentation. Let's take a 10-minute break and then we will be ready to get started."

Everyone stood up to stretch and the gentleman next to Savannah asked if he could get her a cup of coffee. She nodded with a smile and he was gone within moments to get her beverage. She was reminded again about how kind everyone in California was and smiled as he headed out the door on a mission to get his guest some coffee. She decided to take the extra time to get her computer set up and the slide show cued up and ready. Carlie came over to speak briefly to her and explained that the CEO, was a very "hands on" executive and wanted to know everything that was going on with production at all times. She mentioned that he would sit quietly in the back and observe. Savannah nodded in acknowledgement and Carlie went back to her spot at the back of the room.

Authority didn't intimidate Savannah whatsoever. People were people and she was confident in what she was presenting and was sure anyone who saw the presentation would jump at the opportunity to get in at the ground floor.

A few minutes later, as people were settling back in, Savannah was standing at the front of the room looking at the first slide to make sure it was straight. Carlie walked up behind her and said, "Savannah I would like you to meet James our CEO." Savannah turned around and once again was looking straight at Jim!

She felt her face turn the crimson color that always occurred when he was around. He smiled and shook her hand. She didn't know what to say. He looked at her and said, "We are ready when-ever you are." With that he walked to the back of the room and took a seat. Savannah was speechless. The silence in the room was deafening and yet Savannah couldn't open her mouth. The gen-tleman that had brought her coffee looked at her and smiled. It was like he was willing her to start the presentation and do well. Still, she was silent.

Finally Jim "James" asked her a question, which of course he already knew the answer to, and jarred Savannah back to reality. From there she presented her idea complete with all the angles she had told Jim about the night before. She was thankful that she knew the product so well, as she was unable to think clearly right then and went into autopilot to explain the tool her company had created.

At the end of the presentation, everyone applauded both the presentation and the great idea and Carlie ended the meeting with very positive feedback. She told Savannah that they would discuss the project further and make a determination if they felt their company could make and use the product she had just presented. Carlie told her that they would have a definite answer to her company by the end of next week.

Savannah thanked her and everyone for attending and sat down on a nearby chair finally giving in to the throbbing pain in her ankle. As the group said their goodbyes and filed out, Savannah thought about what had just happened. She couldn't decide if she was mad or thankful that Jim hadn't told her who he really was the night before.

Just then he walked up and said, "How are the crutches holding up? You did a good job up there."

"Thank you and fine," she said. Her pride was getting the best of her and anger was the decision that her subconscious had made.

She looked up to find that it was just the two of them in the conference room.

"Why didn't you say something?" she asked embarrassed. He didn't respond.

She was careful with her words as now the decision of her entire company was riding on this man and she didn't want to do anything to mess it up. She knew she was very capable of telling him off but she was smart enough to know that wouldn't be the most brilliant move.

Instead she opted to get away from the situation as quickly as possible saying as little as possible. That option would be the only way she could hold her tongue.

She stood up and mentioned that she had another appointment to get to and thanked him for his time. Then she hobbled past him as quickly as her leg would allow and went out to the receptionist to ask her to call her a cab. She hopped on to the elevator and as the doors were closing she saw Jim running to try to make the elevator. She let the doors close right in front of him.

She was mortified and her eyes started to well up with tears.

She wasn't sure why she was about to cry, she just was, and she desperately tried to get her thoughts collected before the doors opened again. She felt betrayed by Jim and was mad. She always cried when she was really mad, frustrated or scared and today was no exception. Right now she had two of the three emotions going strong and she was losing the battle. Despite trying her hardest, tears began to spill over the rims of her eyes and slid on to her cheeks. As she wiped the tears away, the elevator doors opened and she could see the cab waiting just outside the glass doors.

The sun was shining bright as she positioned herself in the cab and asked the driver to take her for a short ride down to the beachfront. He was happy to do so and it gave her time to think.

Her head was spinning with all the details of the morning and she tried to map out exactly what had occurred. She didn't know if Jim lived in Santa Barbara and was just visiting Lancaster the evening she met him at the club or if he lived in Lancaster, as she had originally thought, and was just here, as she was, on business. *That has to be the case*, she reasoned, as he said they was staying at the same hotel.

The ocean was sparkling in the sunlight and the rushing waves made her momentarily forget her problem and appreciate the beautiful scenery that was right before her eyes. She decided to eat lunch on the beach and asked the cab driver to bring her to the closest restaurant to the water. He did so and she hopped out of the cab and hobbled slowly to the first bench she spotted to rest for a moment.

Her ankle was throbbing. She sat for a few minutes and thought about life while looking at the ocean and thinking about her presentation. She had done a really good job in spite of the last minute curve ball that had been thrown at her and she felt confident that they were going to get the deal. She smiled as she stood up and hopped over to the close by restaurant. She was seated right away at a nice outside table with a view that could only be imagined in Lancaster.

Although she loved clam chowder soup, she decided to try something different and had a tuna melt instead. She didn't really like fish but felt she had to eat *something* from the coast since she was staring at it.

Thoughts went back to how her life was going to change when the product was sold. She figured *The Ripe and Ready Fruit Company* would make the prototype and hopefully purchase the patent. She knew it was going to be sooner rather than later and she felt that she was the one that tipped the hat in their favor.

Savannah had always wanted to volunteer at a center to help children and thought that if she could swing it, she was going to work part-time and devote the other part of her time to helping kids. She felt like she had a lot to offer and knew she could make a difference in a young child's life.

She watched as a group of small children ran playfully through the sand to their mother. Big smiles and tan shoulders told the story of lucky little ones who spent long days on the beach and she thought about the lifetime of memories she was watching transpire right before her eyes.

Once upon a time she had wanted a family but now, at the ripe old age of 28, she thought differently. Since she had been so hurt by Joel, she had removed any possibility of ever having kids as she had sworn off men. Joel had been just like the Dad that she never knew. He was self-centered and in the fast lane – with everything and everyone. He could charm you one minute and pull the rug out from under you the next. She had heard stories about her Dad being the same way although she didn't know the man. He had always been looking for something better and hadn't wanted the burden or the stigma that came with being a father. In his eyes, fathers were old, and he was a player in the truest sense and anything *but* an old man.

She was surprised when she felt a tear escape her eye. She wiped it away quickly wondering why the hurt of Joel, or her Dad for that matter, still caused her heart to ache. She was thankful that she had seen through Joel and had broken off their two and a half year courtship. She had always forgiven his conniving ways but one day, she had just had enough. He had lied to her about being out with a friend. Later that same evening Savannah had run into the friend. He was with his girlfriend and asked where Joel was. She had made some excuse for him but caught the look of terror on his face when he realized that he had just ruined Joel's alibi.

Joel was gone by the end of the week and Savannah had never looked back. Her only regret was that she hadn't been strong enough to end it earlier. She had wasted good years of her life.

Get off the pity pot, she thought. Her mom had raised her well and made sure she was highly educated. She had accomplished that and ended up with a Masters Degree in Marketing. Although her mom had worked two jobs to make ends meet, she always knew where Savannah was and made sure Savannah always did her best. She was a good mom and when she died last year, Savannah thought not only did she lose a wonderful mother; the world lost an amazing human being.

She thought back to that horrible day some preoccupied driver took her mom from her forever. They had just had lunch together and her mom was crossing the street to head back to her car. The distracted driver had been looking down on his cell phone and ran a red light. He hit Savannah's mom as she was walking in the crosswalk. She was killed instantly as the driver had not even realized the light had turned red and had not even tried to stop.

Thankfully, Savannah had not seen the accident as she had walked into the nearby pharmacy when they had parted, to pick up some medicine. She had been telling her mom that she had a headache and her mom had told her that she was working too hard and had to slow down and get a better balance in her life.

"Enjoy life," she had said. "You never know when it will be taken from you!"

Mom had always made her feel good and had always helped her put things into perspective. Her mom had known she was still upset about Joel. She had pointed out that she had a great apartment, and an exciting job that she was fortunate enough to go to every day. "And" she had said with a big smile, "You have *me!*" She had hugged Savannah then, and told her she loved her to pieces (a phrase she always said) and with that she gave Savannah a kiss and she was gone...forever.

Savannah remembered hearing the sirens and thinking about how loud they were and how much they were making her head pound. She paid for her medicine and walked out to see the horrible scene. Her mother was on the ground and the paramedics had just arrived and were taking her vitals. As she ran up to the group, one paramedic had put a blanket over her body and then over her face as well. Savannah had screamed and dropped to her knees. The rest of that day and the weeks that followed were a blur. Ted was there, always by her side, to help her and listen to her. He was a good friend as well as a great boss.

Savannah had earned her position at his company by working hard. She thought about Ted and the wonderful opportunity he had given her. Ted had recognized her work ethic and ability and had promoted her to the Marketing Manager of his start up company. That was why she was here now looking at the beautiful coast of sunny California.

With that thought, she looked again at the ocean thinking that her mom was with her too. It made her happy and she felt at peace. She decided to head back to Lancaster right away as she couldn't really do any sight seeing with her swollen ankle and she was excited to meet with Ted and tell him about the positive outcome of the meeting.

With lunch finished, she stood up with a new sense of purpose and swung her laptop bag over her shoulder. As she turned around to leave, she saw Jim standing right behind her. Once again their eyes met and she was caught by surprise and was tongue-tied.

"Where are you going?" he asked. "You took off out of the building so fast I didn't even have time to ask you if you would like to have lunch. For being on crutches you sure do get around." He looked at her crutches then back at her and smiled.

She just stared at him trying to think quickly. There was no making a fast escape since her crutches were leaning against the chair on the far side of the table. She knew she was mad and she also knew she had to choose her words carefully as she felt the future of her company was riding on the delicate situation she had found herself in.

She decided to play it cool. *I can pretend*, she thought. Pretend that what he thought of her didn't matter to her. But could she pretend the feelings she was feeling for him? That was the part that scared her. She wasn't sure.

She smiled and said "Oh I was on a mission to get down to the beach as soon as possible. I didn't realize you were looking for me." She was hoping he hadn't remembered that she was staring right at him as the doors on the elevator had closed putting a welcome barrier between them at the office and buying her precious time to make her escape.

He just shrugged and said, "Well I am glad I found you. It looks like you have already had lunch."

Savannah then explained that she was going to take a late afternoon flight back to Lancaster.

"I thought you were staying until Sunday?" Jim seemed confused as he tried to put the facts together.

She was surprised at his knowledge but then thought back to the night before when she had told him her original plan of sightseeing in California. She explained that because she had hurt her ankle she thought it best to cut her trip short and return home. She neglected to mention the fact that she wanted to get away from *him*. From his charismatic smile and the unnerving affect he had on her. She was getting lightheaded just thinking about it and she started to sway. He leaned over to help her steady herself but doing that only made things worse. She lost her balance and fell right in to his arms.

He was strong and caught her with ease. As he pulled her upright, he pulled her close, too close for Savannah's comfort, and she had all she could do not to push him harshly away. She was losing it and had to get out of there fast.

He offered to drive her back to the hotel and, because she didn't see a cab around anywhere, she took him up on his offer regretting it immediately after she entered his car. The chemistry between them was electrifying and made her dizzy. She couldn't believe it was only one sided.

The drive to the hotel was awkward, as no one wanted to bring up that their two worlds had collided and they were not prepared. Small talk was disastrous as neither of them was really paying attention to the outward conversation. Each of them seemed to be having a dialogue with their own thoughts and emotions and the air was filled with simple words and canned laughter.

As the car turned the corner and the hotel lobby door was visible, Savannah said, "You can just drop me off in front here. That would be great." Jim was silent for a moment before he spoke.

"I am sorry I didn't tell you what I did for the company. We were having such a good time last night and when we finally started talking about work it took me a few minutes to realize our connection. At that point, I was too selfish I guess, to tell you, and I had a feeling if I had, our evening would have ended quite abruptly or the mood would have changed- kind of like it has now."

The car was stopped at the curb but she didn't make a move to get out. She looked over at him and realized he was right. She was mad that he hadn't told her but, if she thought about it, everything would have been different last night had he told her right away. Instead, they had spent the whole evening talking and laughing and getting to know each other. She had let her guard down with him for some reason and because of that, felt that she needed to get away.

"Can we start over?" Jim asked. This time he didn't make any assumptions that she would do what ever he wanted. He was silent and waiting. Waiting for her decision. Every thought that raced through her head told her to get out of the car. Yet, she couldn't move. It was like she was paralyzed with the realization that she *wanted* to be there and she *wanted* to be with him.

A million thoughts went through her head. She looked over at him, at the twinkling eyes now dimmed by the unknown response to the question he had asked. He waited, just looking at her.

And, against everything that her head told her to do, her voice whispered, "Yes."

CHAPTER FIVE

Savannah and Jim spent the weekend enjoying the beach, eating at quaint little restaurants and talking. Lots and lots of talking. Savannah learned that Jim was adopted and had grown up in Colorado. His parents had been older when they adopted him so Jim's world was centered on adults, mostly family; including an "aunt" that was only 12 years older than he (his Dad's younger sister). He was forever helping his dad work in the garage. They had owned a 5-acre fruit farm that kept them busy. They had customers come to pick fresh seasonal fruit and make a day of it as they had seasonal activities that occurred all year around making the farm a destination for family fun. They also had a small canning operation in the back where the majority of everything grown was canned for later consumption. Jim had spent his life working on those canning lines and had become an expert in mechanical things and how they worked in the process.

The farm was left to him when his parents passed away. Although Jim loved the business, he was searching for more. One spring, right before the summer harvest, their main canning line went down. The small staff was in a panic as the fruit was ripening and they were wondering if they were going to lose the crop. Jim spent more than a few nights researching the cost benefit of getting a whole new line installed or taking his farm in a different direction.

He chose the latter and had become a leader in the field of processing fresh fruit and produce. He was an environmentalist by nature and had developed equipment to process damaged or expired fruit for various other uses including animal food, fertilizer, household cleaning solutions, and was starting to get into the field of creating energy although he hadn't perfected that yet. All products were made to be environmentally friendly and safe to eat at any stage in the process.

Although he kept his fresh fruit and vegetable division going, his heart had moved in the direction of not wasting fruit that was less than perfect. The specialized equipment that he had developed had become the industry standard and at 31, his entrepreneurial spirit had made him a millionaire.

Not that he said those words to Savannah. She just put two and two together. Which brought up the connection as to how they met. Jim owned the company that was looking to make and possibly buy Savannah's company's prototype. It made sense – another use for fruits and vegetables that would allow consumers (both business and residential consumers) to take advantage of eating or using fruits and vegetables to their fullest.

Jim said that his company had locations in several areas throughout the US in order to take advantage of the various crops that grew in the many climates around the country. He was a big proponent of using fresh products and for that reason chose to have smaller facilities that were able to service the surrounding areas.

Jim had been visiting the Lancaster area the night that she had originally met him. He had been called in, as he often was, to review a problem that the Lancaster Ripe and Ready Plant was experiencing. He had been in town for almost a week and had been tired of sitting in his hotel room every night watching TV or looking over work documents. He had made the decision that he needed to get out more and had chosen that evening to do so.

He explained that he had come in to sit and listen to the band and have a drink when he saw the drama unfolding around Savannah. He had noticed her earlier, actually, sitting by herself and had been thinking of going up and introducing himself, but he wasn't very good at small talk. Growing up around adults and then being thrown in to the business world hadn't left a lot of time for college frat parties and socializing with women. In fact, except for seeing his aunt, who was the only relative still alive, he really just immersed himself in his work and did little else.

When he saw the situation with the drunken lady and Savannah, he saw an opportunity and took it. He had been shocked when Savannah just left without even saying goodbye but he chalked it up to "that's how it must be done these days." He had walked around the club a short while later looking for her and when he didn't find the mysterious woman who had already left an impression on him, he left shortly afterward. Although he had thought about her quite a bit since that night, he figured he would never see her again and he needed to get over her. But still, there had been something about her that he just couldn't stop thinking about.

Jim mentioned that his company had plants that spanned as far east as Pennsylvania and west to the coastline of California. Although he spent most of the time in his hometown of Boulder, Colorado, he enjoyed traveling to the various plants throughout the country. He was a very hands-on owner and was involved in any big decision or company venture his company embarked on.

Savannah was truly impressed. Not because he was so very successful but because his humble background allowed him to be a genuinely caring person. Although he had not had the perfect traditional family life, he had risen above any obstacle thrown at him and had been amazingly successful in the process. The weekend flew by and before they both knew it, Sunday afternoon had arrived and Savannah had a plane to catch. Jim was scheduled to stay in California for another week before heading back to Boulder.

Saying goodbye was as hard as it was awkward. Although they had come close, there had been no physical contact whatsoever and the powerful energy that seemed to be pushing them together was an exhausting fight to overcome. Savannah had vowed to keep her personal life separate from her professional life and that internal decision had kept the wall securely around her emotions, although her heart and body were telling a different story.

A generic hug ended their weekend encounter and she hobbled up the runway feeling tears starting to well up in her eyes. She looked back to see the man that had awakened her heart fading from sight as he too looked back at her. Their eyes met and once again, the feelings that she had tried to bury ripped through to her very core.

She took her seat by the window and wondered if she would ever see Jim again. She also wondered how things would work if his company decided to purchase and build the prototype for her company. Would he be around more? If she saw him would it be strictly on a business level? Is that how it would have to be? Is that what she wanted?

For the first time since the weekend had started, she actually didn't know what she wanted more – the company prototype to be purchased – or Jim. She felt relieved the choice wasn't hers to make.

CHAPTER SIX

Savannah was anxious to get in to work on Monday. She had texted her boss, Ted, as soon as the plane had landed back in Lancaster. He had called her right away and she gave him every detail of the meeting. She left out the part about her "getting to know" the owner as she didn't want her boss to think that, if they purchased the prototype, it was because of the relationship that had sort of formed. She knew the product was good and would be purchased based on its own merit and not any other factor.

She had spent the rest of Sunday night unpacking and thinking about Jim, exactly what she hadn't wanted to do. Her ankle was much better although she still felt better leaning on one crutch. She had put a call in to Trish but she hadn't picked up. She had tried to stay busy but the evening seemed to drag. She didn't expect that Jim would call her because she hadn't given him her cell number and, come to think of it, he hadn't even asked. At that realization Savannah had been crushed and tossed and turned in bed all night.

Monday morning had not come soon enough. Everyone was smiling as she hobbled past them in the hallway and she wondered if her boss had said anything. *We don't have the agreement yet,* she thought. *We can't get our hopes up.*

Ted walked in to her office before she could even put her purse down. She laid her crutches against the wall and hopped over to her chair behind her desk. He had a twinkle in his eye like he had a secret to tell. He sat across from her now and looked at her with a big grin.

"So, I hear you had help after you fell at the airport." Savannah felt like a spotlight had been pointed in her direction and it was her turn to recite the next line. Instead she just gave him a blank stare, as she really didn't know what to say.

"The airline staff called to give me your information, along with your "caregiver's" information at your request," he said. "They had been instructed by you to let your company know which urgent care you were going to and with whom you were going. Did you have any idea who you were with?"

Savannah looked at Ted with a puzzled look and then laughed as the pieces fell in to place.

"No," she said with a smile. "I had no idea who my caregiver was at the time that I asked for the airline staff to let someone know where I was going. In fact, I didn't make the connection of who he was until after my presentation if you can believe that!"

Ted then asked a million questions – not so much about the presentation but about the CEO of the company that seemed to be holding all the cards for the sale of the product. Savannah thought that was interesting.

She found it interesting too that he hadn't asked so much *about* Jim but about what *she* thought of Jim and the kind of person he was. Ted had been like a father to Savannah and, right now, seemed more like a father figure than a boss.

Ted had always admired the way she could read people and know the kind of person they were after meeting them for just a short time. She had proven her skill on a couple of different occasions when she had sat in on interviews and had a negative sense about somebody. On both the occasions, Ted had hired the person anyway thinking that Savannah had been way off, only to be proven wrong later realizing that she had been right on with her gut feeling. Savannah smiled and said she thought Jim was nice and tried to turn the conversation back to the presentation and the encouraging words that Carlie, the Project Manager, had said. Just then Savannah's assistant rang through on the phone and asked if Ted was available. There was a call holding for him on line three. Savannah was just about to ask Ted what he knew about the company. Was he willing to put his cherished idea into the hands of a group of people they didn't really know?

Ted smiled and got up. He winked at Savannah and left her office and she wasn't sure what to make of the whole thing. Was this *the* call that everyone had been waiting for? Was her life about to change? Was everyone's life about to change? She could see through the window that the assistant was excited as Ted walked by. Others in the area seemed to be moving quickly as they mulled around the assistant's desk to wait for the results of the phone call.

Savannah, on the other hand was sick to her stomach. She no longer knew what she wanted. And, she was concerned about the questions Ted had been asking her about Jim – and about his character. What did he know that he didn't tell her? Was he keeping something from her or had they been interrupted by a phone call?

Ted didn't come back to her office after the phone call. *Maybe it wasn't Carlie* thought Savannah. *Maybe it was someone calling in sick.* The assistant had gone back to her work and everyone seemed to be back to a normal working pace – whatever that was.

She was surprised that Ted wasn't in his office when she stopped by before lunch as he always ate lunch at his desk. She had plans to meet Trish but had decided to stop by his office before hand to get updated. No such luck and she thought that odd as she left the building and made her way out in the chilly fall afternoon. She thought about how perfect the weather had been in California. The weather was perfect, the people were nice, and Jim was there...

She shivered and walked in to the corner coffee shop where she and Trish always met. They had a lot of catching up to do. She hadn't talked to her since the quick phone call when Trish had cancelled on going to California and had told her the exciting news about her engagement. Trish had wanted to tell Savannah about Bill – how he had proposed and about their wedding plans. They were embarking on very unfamiliar territory to Savannah and she hoped she could stay focused for Trish's sake. But her heart wasn't in it. It was back in California.

CHAPTER SEVEN

Lunch with Trish was exciting as she and Bill had made plans to marry in late winter or early spring and Trish had asked Savannah to be her Maid of Honor. They talked about color themes and venues and Trish had said that although it was going to be a small wedding – no more than 50 – venues filled up fast and she and Bill had just about decided on the location. She said she would keep Savannah posted and they agreed to meet again soon to talk about her plans. Savannah wanted to help as much as possible and was so excited she forgot all about the unanswered questions back at work and the phone call that had taken Ted away from her.

As soon as Savannah walked through the doors of her office building after lunch she immediately remembered the flurry of questions she had for Ted. She went to his office hoping to find him there but again he was out of office, which was not like him. His assistant said that he was in off-site meetings and would be gone for the rest of the afternoon. Savannah looked closely to see if the assistant knew something that she wasn't sharing but there was no hint of secrecy in her eyes so Savannah went back to her office.

The rest of the afternoon flew by, as she was busy playing catch up from the few days she had missed. She was in charge of a group of three people and it always amazed her at how much work was generated for her by such a small group. The pamphlets and other documentation they had created had been an important part of their invitation to present their product. She and her team had also done extensive research to find out which companies could use or might have an interest in their product. When they had contacted *The Ripe and Ready Fruit Company*, they had received a positive response. Ted had taken it from there and had secured the presentation date and time.

Before long it was 5:00 p.m. and she decided to call it a day. She left, along with a few others, and stopped to get some Chinese take-out on her way home. The restaurant was right next door to her office and it was her favorite. As she walked out of the restaurant, to-go container in one hand, her purse, brief case, and the crutch to assist her under her other arm, she looked up to see that the sun had already started down in the sky. She had thought about catching a bus or a taxi due to her ankle but she really felt like walking. The air was cool and she had no other plans. She really didn't live that far as her apartment was located downtown. Her apartment was nestled in a mixed-use area of a newly developed part of the city. Although her place was about a 20-minute walk from her office, today she knew it would take her twice as long if not longer. She decided to start walking and, if necessary, catch a cab if she got too tired.

She loved that her home was close to everything and she smiled remembering how lucky she had been to get the last vacant apartment upon its grand opening a year and a half ago. It had been the one bright light in the dismal time after the break up with Joel. Although Joel had moved out of their shared apartment, she hadn't wanted to live there alone with all of the memories. She had been out walking one day and happened to see a sign in the upstairs window of the apartment located above a group of two small restaurants and a small clothing store that sold contemporary fashions.

It was perfect. A nice new one bedroom apartment with all the modern bells and whistles including hardwood floor, updated paint colors, crown molding and a beautiful cut-out bay window which overlooked the busy city street. The kitchen was small but bright and airy with stainless steel appliances and granite counter tops. The unit had been discounted due to a smaller bathroom compared to the other units. Savannah fell in love with it and put a deposit on it that day. She was moved two weeks later.

Tonight, as she made her way home, she thought about the first apartment she had shared with Joel. They had lived together after knowing each other for less than a year. Big mistake. She had tried to be the perfect "roommate" but it seemed like he didn't care. He was careless and left his stuff everywhere. He expected Savannah to wait on him hand and foot but wasn't ready to return the favor. She made a nice dinner every night, and then had to do the dishes as well. He never offered to help and after awhile she quit asking him. They argued often and their home was never comfortable to her. She always felt on edge, almost like she was waiting for the other shoe to drop. She winced as she remembered those awful times and asked herself again, why she had waited so long before she ended the relationship. She had wished she had broken it off much earlier. It might have prevented the dark stain she now had on her heart.

It's o.k., she thought. *I am on the other side of that mess and I have everything to be thankful for.* She hobbled through the doorway of her apartment and turned on the heater. She wished she had a fireplace but that was the other drawback to this unit. She shivered as she saw the wind picking up outside. She wondered if winter was going to make its appearance sooner this year. Last year it had been unseasonably cold with more snow falling then they had ever experienced. The snow had arrived a little late but had been constant and seemed to last until well into spring. She was hoping for a more mild winter this year.

After eating, Savannah went to change. She smiled as she put on the same yoga pants she had worn when Jim had stopped by her hotel room. She remembered how awkward she had felt when she opened the door and how, less than an hour later they had been talking as if they had known each other for years. Savannah glanced at her leg, which was sore and a little swollen, but was healing nicely. *Thank God,* she thought. She had only used both crutches until she returned home and from that point on, she had tried using one crutch and had been successful. She had taken it slow, had worn flat shoes and had been able to get around pretty well. She sat down on the couch, turned on the TV and elevated her leg.

Just then her cell phone rang which startled her and she jumped. She looked down to see a blocked call. *Telemarketer,* she thought and didn't answer it. It wasn't until the last ring that it dawned on her that it might be Jim. She grabbed the phone and tried to "slide to unlock" as the "smart" phone directed her to do but she couldn't do it fast enough. The phone stopped ringing and she had missed the call. She waited to see if a voicemail would appear but it didn't.

She fell asleep that night with a heavy heart. Something was bothering her but she couldn't put her finger on it. Was it the fact that Jim hadn't called or was it the fact that Ted had made her feel so uneasy about him? Was it Jim, or his company or both? Their company was about to take off because as soon as that prototype was made, the product would be sold and, if *The Ripe and Ready Fruit Company* purchased the patent, Jim's marketing team would be advertising it all over the country. Very soon life could change. It was a little unnerving and Savannah wasn't sure she was ready for her life to change so drastically even though this is what they had all been working so hard for.

CHAPTER EIGHT

It was late and Ted was sitting, staring blankly at the fire crackling loudly in his fireplace. His wife, Bette, had gone to bed some time ago but for some reason he couldn't sleep. He was hoping that the loud crackling noise of the newly added log to the fire wouldn't wake her.

He was thinking about the phone call he had received from Carlie, the Project Manager at *The Ripe and Ready Fruit Company,* and the proposal she had presented for their prototype. He couldn't believe it. His dream was coming true. Why did he now have this sixth sense that something wasn't right? He had never had this feeling before and had always admired Savannah's intuition but, after their conversation earlier today, he felt she hadn't received any warning signals. So why was he getting them?

He went over the details again in his mind. Carlie had said that upper management had met and decided that their product was one that could be used both commercially as well as in private homes and would definitely be something *The Ripe and Ready Fruit Company* could personally use and market. She had asked if they were willing to sit down with both company attorneys to negotiate a deal. She didn't have the exact numbers but she was looking at an initial payout of two million with an additional one million payout per year for the immediate three years following the release. They, of course, would have ownership of the product name and patent. She had mentioned that her company, because of its nature, could use and market the product to its fullest.

A meeting had been scheduled for the end of the month, as their attorney was out of town and wouldn't be returning until then. Their company attorney, James (Jim) and Carlie would fly to Lancaster to put the finishing touches on the contract and prepare it for signature. If everything went as planned, they hoped to begin production the first week in January of next year.

It was all happening so fast that Ted wasn't quite sure what to do. He had played off the call casually to his assistant saying that they had just wanted some general information and kept a poker face to mask his excitement – or was it concern? He had to leave the office right away, as he knew if Savannah saw him, it would be all over. He wasn't good at keeping secrets and she could read him like a book. He had driven to the library to do some research on *The Ripe and Ready Fruit Company* to see if he could get positive information to shake this uncomfortable feeling he was having.

He had found only positive posts about the products, service and staff of the company. Content with the findings, he had tried to shake off the bad vibes he was feeling and concentrate on his ride home. A chill was in the air and the wind was really picking up. He wondered if this winter was going to be anything like last winter. He remembered how crazy the snow had been and how one night last winter the entire staff had ended up spending the night after getting snowed in. They all had a great time and got along really well.

With the sale of the company, he knew that the wonderful group of people at work would disband and go their separate ways. It was sad to think about. Maybe that was what was bothering him. He would just have to wait and see.

CHAPTER NINE

Savannah woke up to a buzzing phone. She looked at the caller ID but this time didn't hesitate to pick up the call knowing full well it could be Jim. She glanced at the clock next to her bed as it clicked to 12:31 a.m. It seems like she had just fallen asleep even though she had nodded off around 10:15 p.m.

A remorseful Jim was on the other end apologizing for the thoughtlessness of forgetting about the time difference. He had left an evening meeting early to call her and had completely forgotten about the time difference until he had heard the sleepiness in her voice. He had debated whether or not to hang up but ended up talking anyway. She quickly recovered from her haziness and her next words spoken were like she had been up for hours. He asked how her flight had been and also asked about her ankle. She recognized how thoughtful he was and smiled.

They ended up talking for hours about anything and everything. They talked about their likes and desires, about their dislikes and fears. They shared things with each other that neither of them had ever shared with anyone before and acknowledged that, with each of them being an only child, they had missed out on that special bond that siblings seemed to share.

They talked about the weather, their cars (or in Savannah's

case her dream car since she didn't have one) and where they wanted to live someday. After over two hours the call ended with Jim saying he would call her tomorrow evening at 8:00 p.m. *her* time.

She hung up the phone and realized her phone battery was almost dead. As she drifted off to sleep she thought about their chance meeting at the club and the irony that Trish's ticket had ended up with him. She also thought about how they hadn't talked about business at all.

When she thought about it, it seemed strange but then she put those thoughts out of her head as she thought about all the things Jim had told her about himself. She couldn't believe how much they were alike even though they had grown up in different parts of the country and with very different backgrounds. She really believed in fate and thought that fate had definitely had a role in their coming together.

The rest of the week was filled with phone calls and the weekend with face time, which she loved. Monday morning came too fast. All she could think about was Jim. She felt like she was falling in love with this man and wondered if people could really fall in love so fast. She looked up love versus infatuation on line and discovered it was really too early to tell what it was that she felt.

She decided to stop analyzing her feelings and just enjoy them. Jim was flying in to Lancaster on Wednesday to visit his plant and they had plans to meet that evening for dinner. She was so excited and couldn't wait to tell Trish about him. She had mentioned him off handedly, when she and Trish had met for lunch, but she didn't want to monopolize the conversation. It was a time for Trish to shine and wasn't and shouldn't have been about her.

Tuesday morning Savannah decided to take a taxi to work, as it had been raining really hard and she didn't want to take any chances of getting sick before Wednesday. She hadn't anticipated taking a cab as she had been planning to do her usual walk. Her ankle was much better and she wanted to continue to strengthen it. When she had gotten outside she noticed the rain and hailed a cab. Now she had arrived at work early and decided to go in and get a jump-start on the day. As she walked down the hall, she noticed the light on in Ted's office and remembered that they hadn't had any closure to the Monday phone call that had occurred the week before. She had thought it odd that she hadn't run in to Ted all last week or yesterday either. She popped her head in to say hi and startled Ted. He looked tired and worn out.

"Is everything ok?" she questioned. Ted smiled weakly and said that everything was fine.

She asked about the phone call that had interrupted their conversation the week before and Ted managed to recite the same line he had told his assistant last week. Normally Savannah would have seen right through the lie but today she was so distracted with her newfound love that she wasn't thinking straight. She accepted what he said and didn't think any more about it.

Instead she decided to press Ted for why he had questioned her so much about Jim. He explained that he felt that she was a good judge of character and that he valued her opinion. Savannah opened up a little more and told him what she had learned about Jim. Everything pointed to the fact that Jim was who he said he was and his story had mirrored pretty much what Ted had learned about him online. Ted then asked about the main headquarters, how many people worked there, what the office was like and if the company was as big as it seemed to be. He asked about the different levels of staff and whom she had met. He also asked what she thought about Carlie and if she was the only project manager or one of many.

Savannah described a beautiful glass building that was three stories high and had a distant view of the ocean. She said the floor that she had visited had been well furnished and was known as Mahogany Square. That floor was where the upper level management had their offices as well as the company's conference room. There seemed to be at least 100 people in the building, she assumed, because although she had only been to the top floor, she explained that she had noticed that the first floor was for production and the second floor was for the rest of the office staff. The parking lot had been full. Savannah also explained that the building wasn't large but seemed tall probably because of the glass windows. She said that the group of people that had been in attendance during the presentation were very nice and of varying ages (both men and women). They appeared to be interested in her product and asked all the right questions. She said she hadn't spoken to Carlie too much herself but got the sense from the group that she was well respected. She had carried herself well and was confident and helpful. She wasn't sure if there were other project managers or exactly how the company was structured.

Ted then asked if he she had any weird vibe about the place at all. Savannah didn't even question why he asked but was quick to say no as she truly hadn't gotten any negative feelings about the company, the people, Santa Barbara or California, come to think of it.

She told Ted that Jim was coming in to town tomorrow to visit the Lancaster Plant and they were going to have dinner. She asked, out of respect, if Ted would like to join them but he bowed out gracefully saying he had another commitment that night. Savannah stood up and smiled and said she would bring him by to introduce him before they left. She left his office then, and Ted wondered why Savannah hadn't asked him about the deal and what they were going to do. She seemed a little giddy as she talked about Jim.

Maybe she doesn't know about the deal, he thought. *I wonder why Jim hasn't said anything about it to her.* He liked Jim already. He was keeping his business life and his personal life separate. *Good for him.* Just then, another thought occurred to Ted. *Did Jim and Savannah have an attraction to each other? Why were they meeting for dinner?* He started to become a little suspicious but reasoned that Jim knew that Savannah was not the deciding factor of the company, *he* was and he intended to do all his homework before splitting up his "family." And, making everyone rich in the process.

CHAPTER TEN

Jim's plane landed at 3:05 p.m. Wednesday afternoon. By 5:30 p.m. he was walking up the pathway to Savannah's office just as several employees were filing out. They were dodging the rain that had just started falling and commented on how cold it already was for late October. It was dark out, and with the chilling cold wind blowing strong, Jim was thankful for the unlocked door as he opened it and walked in to the warm lobby. He had texted Savannah as his taxi pulled up and now he could hear the clicking of heels walking down the hall. He was really looking forward to seeing Savannah. She had been all he could think about since they had officially met two weeks ago in California and he thought it strange that he would reconnect with the woman who caught his eye the last time he had been in Lancaster two months earlier. After that chance meeting on the dance floor, he had thought about her many times and had even told a couple of his colleagues about his connection with a women that took his breath away – and then was gone. His heart jumped a little when Savannah turned the corner and he once again was staring into those beautiful brown eyes. She looked unbelievable. She was wearing a brown straight skirt that stopped just above her knees. She wore a cream colored silky top that was tucked in to her skirt and showed off her figure. Her brown pumps made her look taller than he had remembered and a big chunky necklace completed her outfit.

She smiled a little shyly and welcomed him with a friendly hug. He leaned down, as he was still so much taller even with her heels and the smell of her perfume captivated him further. She felt comfortable in his arms and he was happy she had invited him over to her office.

"I want you to meet my boss before we go, is that ok?" He nodded and they walked side by side down the hallway to the door with the light shining out.

"Ted, this is Jim from *The Ripe and Ready Fruit Company*. Jim, this is Ted, my Boss." Savannah's introductions were on a professional level but each knew the deeper level of their relationship with Savannah.

Savannah had told Jim that Ted had been like the father she had never had, and they had known each other for years. Her mom had worked for Ted in his prior company and he had watched Savannah grow into a nice young lady. He had been around a lot as he, his wife Bette and Savannah's mother were good friends and had been very close. When Savannah's father had taken off for the last time and her mother had been left with nothing, Ted had helped her pick up the pieces and he and Bette had been there to help care for Savannah. He had especially been there for her when her mother had passed and had told her if she ever needed anything, she need only ask.

Savannah had given Ted a little more information about Jim earlier in the day and had shared bits and pieces about what she had learned about him. Ted could tell now, from the sparkle in her eye, that this guy was someone pretty special although in his mind he continued to question why Jim hadn't mentioned a word about the acquisition of the company to Savannah. If Jim was the owner, as Ted believed he was, why didn't he talk business, even now?

Savannah and Jim had been talking amongst themselves as Ted pondered this question and Savannah turned to Ted to say her goodbyes. The smile on her face was radiant. Jim too had a smile that matched Savannah's as he said good-bye and turned to leave.

Jim reached for Savannah's hand as they walked out the door and Savannah's face turned a brilliant shade of red.

It dawned on Ted then, that Jim was under the same spell that Savannah was under. Work was the *last* thing on their mind even though it had been the very thing they had brought them together.

CHAPTER ELEVEN

Jim was in town until Sunday. He had work to do on Thursday and Friday but the evenings were spent with Savannah. They had dinner with Trish and Bill one night and, when Savannah texted Trish later after Jim had dropped her off, Trish had called her right away. She told Savannah that she really liked him and Bill thought he was a good guy as well. Trish could tell that he was something special to Savannah and she was really happy for her.

The weekend was filled with sight seeing, talking and getting to know each other as intimately as possible. They had both decided to take their physical relationship slow and by doing so had made every meeting that much more electrifying. When they finally consummated their feelings on Sunday before Jim left, it was the stuff songs were made from. The uninhibited passion that they both experienced made for a lovemaking session that left them both breathless and wanting for more.

Savannah had never imagined such a connection. Especially since she hadn't had anywhere near it with Joel. And, although Jim had had many experiences over the years, no one had even come close to making him feel what he had experienced with Savannah.

Jim left Sunday night and Savannah was heartbroken. She missed him already and couldn't wait to see him again. Jim mentioned that something was in the works and he would be back in town by the end of November.

Savannah had asked for more details at that time but Jim hadn't had any, saying they were still working out some numbers and he really wasn't at liberty to say. Savannah respected his position and didn't badger him.

Ted called her into the office Monday afternoon as everyone was leaving for the day. He then told her about the phone call he had received from Carlie and about the tentative offer that was in the works. Savannah was in shock. It was finally coming true. Ted explained that he had done a lot of research about the company and everything had checked out. He felt that if both attorneys agreed to everything (they had already both been provided a copy of the offer) then papers would be signed by the end of the month.

Savannah asked if Jim had been involved in the negotiation as well. Ted told her that his understanding was that he makes the overall investments but it is up to his staff and the attorneys to negotiate all the details. At that point he steps away from the deal. Savannah smiled as she remembered how Jim had mentioned something was in the works but hadn't really given any details. *Probably because he hadn't had them,* she thought.

Although everyone was going to make a lot of money on the deal, anyone who still wanted to work would have a job at the Lancaster Ripe and Ready Fruit Plant. The prototype was to be made at the Santa Barbara headquarters location however, and they had asked that Ted and his top-level staff relocate to California for about a year – maybe longer. This would ensure the design would be done correctly and the product would work efficiently. The one-year relocation was part of the package. Ted had mentioned this to her because obviously Savannah was one of the key staff members along with Bob, in Engineering, and himself. He then asked Savannah if she was ready to pickup and move.

Savannah thought about it for a minute. Hmm, a year in sunny California. What was there to think about? She didn't have any family here and her closest friend was getting married soon and was definitely preoccupied. Her other closest companion was Ted and it sounded like he and his wife would be going too. Just then Savannah looked up at Ted and, as if he read her mind, he said, "Yes, Bette and I will be going as well. Bob, I am not so sure about. He has a wife and kids to think about. He might just take the package and move on. I already mentioned that they might not get all three of us. They were ok with just the two of us as Carlie told me that they have a highly skilled engineer already on staff."

Savannah nodded and smiled. She was looking past Ted as if in a trance. She was trying to take it all in.

"When would we need to move?" she asked.

"After the first of the year," he said. Savannah thought about it for a moment. All kinds of things were running through her mind and then Trish's wedding popped in to her head. *What about Trish's wedding?* She wondered. *I believe she said it was going to be in the spring.* She desperately wanted to be there for her best friend. She knew that flights were expensive and it would be hard to fly back and forth.

That of course was the down side of the move. The upside of the move would be moving to California and having the opportunity to spend more time with Jim. That alone made the decision seem like a no-brainer.

CHAPTER TWELVE

Ted suddenly felt relieved and felt good about the decision. Savannah had been excited and asked for much more detailed information about the sale, the process and the next steps once the initial shock of it all had worn off.

Ted spoke to Bob and presented the opportunity to see if he was interested. As Ted had guessed, Bob turned down the relocation due to family commitments. He had kids in school and a wife whose own career was flourishing. They were not in a position to pick up and move. Instead, Bob asked if he would possibly be able to head up the Engineering Department at the Ripe and Ready Fruit Plant in Lancaster.

Ted had explained that he did not have that kind of authority but would propose that suggestion to Carlie and the rest of the negotiating team during the last bit of discussions and meetings regarding the sale of the company. Ted had asked that Bob not mention anything to staff until after the paperwork was done and the sale was a done deal. He would then have a company wide meeting, followed by a huge celebratory party. Bob was a good guy and Ted knew that his secret was safe.

Meanwhile the first couple of weeks in November had been hectic. Ted and Savannah had worked for hours on end putting a timeline together of the move process and making sure that procedures for everything they had worked so hard to create were accurate and efficient. They did research on how companies shut down operations and what the protocol was for employee severance.

Because the company hadn't "gone public" which had been the goal when the product was first created, the payout to employees was going to be different than offering employees lots of great stock options. Ted wanted to make sure that the employees were well rewarded for their efforts.

The final meeting with Jim, Carlie, Ted and attorneys for both sides took place the last week of November right before the Thanksgiving holiday. It had started snowing in Lancaster and Carlie commented on the "asset" of nice weather that both Ted and Savannah would be receiving as part of the temporary relocation package. Everyone had laughed and agreed, although when Ted told Savannah about the comment later on, she thought about it and said she would miss the possibility of holidays covered in white.

The meeting was positive and ended with a champagne toast as both parties stood up and shook hands. It was a win-win situation and everyone was excited and anxious to get started. Ted felt that he had accomplished what he had set out to do, which was to make a useful product for the world.

The move date was scheduled for the last week of February, as the production area was being remodeled and the space that they would be using wouldn't be available until then. Ted and Savannah would have offices on the third floor, the floor that Savannah had originally visited.

When Savannah heard about the start date she was ecstatic. Trish had amazingly decided to get married on Valentines Day so the timing was perfect! Savannah would be able to stay in town to help her with final wedding preparations, throw her a wedding shower and go somewhere fun for her bachelorette party.

What Savannah hadn't known was that Trish knew that Savannah would be moving soon and she really wanted to make sure Savannah would be able to be a part of her wedding. She and Bill had discussed it and they had decided to get married earlier than planned. They paid the premium rate to get married *on* Valentine's Day to make sure that Savannah could be at the wedding. Bill did it for Trish. Trish did it for Savannah. Savannah never knew the true reason behind the Valentine's Day wedding.

CHAPTER THIRTEEN

Jim and Savannah had become quite an item. They skyped every night and Jim would fly to Lancaster every chance he got. For as close as they had become, they had decided that they were not going to tell anyone other than a few close friends which included Ted and Bette, about their relationship until after the year long merging process was complete. Savannah didn't want Carlie to know either. Savannah had mentioned to Jim she didn't want any weird feelings between herself and the staff project manager and he understood.

Jim spent Thanksgiving with Savannah and they ended up going to Ted and Bette's house to celebrate. Ted and Bette's kids were grown and didn't live in the area. Jim and Savannah had a great time and Savannah was glad that Ted and Jim got along so well. There was no "shop talk" the whole day. Instead they played board games, ate a huge turkey dinner and sat around the fire drinking wine and talking about Savannah's childhood. Savannah enjoyed hearing her memories from a different viewpoint and she thought it interesting that Jim was listening so intently.

She didn't think Joel knew anything about her childhood or even cared for that matter.

Christmas time came and was filled with a flurry of events that included the company Christmas party/company sale party. It was held at the new Spanish style hotel that had just opened on the west side of town. The venue was beautiful, the food was exquisite and everyone had a great time. Company bonuses were handed out and as the evening was coming to a close, it was bittersweet as staff knew that their "family" would soon be moving on and going their separate ways. The final compensation check was to be included as part of their last check in February. Ted had held a meeting the first week of December to let everyone know what was happening. He figured it would give people a couple of months to start looking for a new job although every one of the nearly 50 people would have enough money to tide them over for a very long time. Although it had been Ted's company, he shared the sale very generously as his belief was a person should never have more money then he knew what to do with. As it was, he planned on donating a lot of his money to the various charities that both he and Bette were passionate about. He hadn't exactly narrowed down specifics yet, but he and Bette had talked about it, and after making sure their kids and grandkids were set, they figured it was the right thing to do.

Jim had not attended the party as he had been stuck at the Colorado plant trying to defuse another problem. It worked out fine, because it helped keep the relationship between Savannah and Jim quiet. They felt strongly that it was better that way.

As the holiday season was winding down, it seemed that a chapter was closing in Savannah's life. The weather had been unreasonably bad and she kept envisioning how wonderful life would be in California. She checked the Lancaster forecast daily on her phone noting that it was raining, snowing or just plain freezing. Only moderate temperature changes were occurring in her future homeland and for that she was very grateful.

She and Trish had put the final touches on her wedding and Trish's bachelorette party was planned for the last weekend in January. There would be six of them going across the border to New York for a weekend of fun, fun, fun. They were leaving late Friday afternoon and would spend their weekend at a posh hotel located near Times Square. They had reservations to see a Broadway show, something Trish had always wanted to do. Saturday would be spent shopping, getting hair and nails done, and getting ready for a night on the town. They were eating at one of the new hip downtown restaurants and then would go clubbing the rest of the evening. Sunday would be spent sleeping, enjoying Sunday brunch and heading back home.

Trish's bridal shower had been scheduled for the first weekend in February, just a week before the wedding. Although Savannah thought they were cramming everything together, Trish's sister was going to be flying in from Florida and hadn't been able to come out any sooner. She had small children and had to make arrangements to take time off of work. She really wanted to be there and she and her family would just stay the week and attend the wedding the following weekend. That way she only had to pay round trip airfare for everyone once.

Savannah had calculated that she had exactly three weeks in January and two weeks in February to pack her 28 years up and get ready to move. She had a feeling that she wouldn't ever be coming back to Lancaster, at least not to live. With all the events going on over the next five weeks, she would have to use her time wisely and be very organized.

Jim's company had agreed to set them up in a condominium complex and had paid a one-year lease for Ted and Bette as well as Savannah. She had seen pictures of her new place and she was excited at the possibilities that lay ahead of her. Since it was completely furnished, she knew she didn't need a whole lot of things and had decided to sell or give away everything she could. When it was all said and done, she was surprised at how few material things really meant enough to her to keep and carry them across country.

Jim, although his home base was still in Colorado, also had a unit in the condo complex, and Savannah figured she would be seeing a lot more of him. This, of course, added to the excitement of her new life. When she had first heard that Jim had a condo in the same complex where they were being housed, Savannah had asked Jim why he had been staying in the hotel she was at when they first met at the airport. He laughed then, and explained he wasn't staying there but he had needed to act quickly and come up with an excuse to help her or she wouldn't have let him. He smiled and said, "It was the only thing I could think of at the time." Savannah thought about it and figured the timing was about right. He had gotten all her information, room number, etc. went home and changed and was back after grabbing a bottle of wine and getting a quick bite to eat. *Come to think of it*, she thought, *he didn't have any bags with him from the plane other then a little carry on.* Wow, how had she missed that?

She was looking forward to her new life. The most important thing that both she and Jim had to remember for now was that they were going to keep their relationship quiet. It created another layer of excitement as they talked about how they would find creative ways to sneak around. It made their relationship even more electrifying if that were even possible.

CHAPTER
FOURTEEN

Valentine's Day dawned and the city was wrapped in a white blanket of snow. Trish's wedding took place in a quaint little chapel surrounded by snow-capped rolling hills. The sun was sparkling for the 11:30 a.m. wedding which made for a truly picturesque scene. The reception was at a close by Italian Villa that smelled of warm garlic bread and beautiful flowers. The day went off without a hitch and as Trish and Bill left for their honeymoon, Savannah hoped and prayed they would forever be as happy as they looked at the moment.

Savannah would be gone before they got back from their honeymoon so their goodbye was filled with tears and memories and promises to get together and keep in touch. On the one hand, Savannah was leaving one of the most important people in her life. She was heartbroken. On the other hand, she had a whole new life waiting for her in California with her good friend Ted and his wife and, most importantly, Jim. She and Jim had enjoyed the wedding and were looking forward to a wonderful Valentine celebration of their own. She still had her apartment until Wednesday morning, the day of her flight, and together they spent Sunday and Monday morning wrapping up last minute details for Savannah's departure. Ted's company was officially closed and other than saying goodbye to her neighbors at the apartment complex, everything was done.

Wednesday morning arrived and with bags packed and a one-way ticket purchased, Savannah boarded the plane with a heavy heart. She was traveling alone as Jim had left late Monday afternoon for a meeting in Colorado, and Ted and Bette would be leaving at the end of the week, as they had to wrap up the details of their house. They had rented it out to a very nice couple with the idea that they would be back as soon as the one-year commitment was over. Savannah knew that she would probably never be back even if things didn't work out for her and Jim. She had been bitten by the California bug and had decided that California was going to be her permanent home.

The plane ride was so different from the last time she had flown out west. It wasn't as crowded for some reason. There was not even a chance to strike up a conversation with the person sitting next to her, as the two seats in her row were empty. *Oh well,* she thought. *It will give me a chance to think about what I want to do first when I get to my new home.*

She didn't have to report to work until Monday morning, which gave her the rest of the week to unpack and get settled. Jim wouldn't be in California until late Friday evening and had said he would come to her place when he arrived.

As the plane wheels touched down in California, she looked out the window and smiled. She felt so confident and happy. Very different from how she had felt just five months earlier. So much had happened. A quick summary of the events flashed through her mind and she suddenly remembered her abrupt debarking of the plane. She was careful not to repeat that mistake. As the cool breeze from the walkway hit her face, she smiled remembering the freezing temperature she had just left. Life was good.

CHAPTER
FIFTEEN

A staff member from her new workplace was there to greet her and bring her to the condominium complex. She had said that she didn't need a car right away and she and Jim had talked about how he would help her get a car as soon as she was settled. In the meantime, there were so many places she could walk to that it hardly seemed necessary. The cold wasn't even *that* cold and she thought that she must be in heaven.

Jim called her that evening to make sure she had gotten to her new place with no issues. She had unpacked the few suitcases she had brought and with the furnishings already in place, had little to do once the suitcases were empty. She sighed as she unpacked realizing once again that she really didn't have that much to show for her 28 years of life. There were only a few precious items that had made the cut to move west with her.

She shrugged off the sad thoughts and decided that tomorrow she was going to take a walk and see what her new neighborhood had in store for her. Jim had laughed at her excitement to go exploring. She had told him about a book she had purchased at the airport outlining the sights of Santa Barbara and now she set-tled down to read and learn more about her new hometown.

Thursday morning came quickly and she was surprised to see the sun peeking through the window. A bright sunny day in Feb-ruary. She smiled, put on her warm bathrobe and slippers and shuffled into the kitchen. Her kitchen was small but very bright. It wasn't as updated as the apartment she had just left but she loved the soft yellow color of the walls and her head was already filling up with ideas for decorative accents that would make the kitchen feel cozy. The living room was spacious and had a wood-burning fireplace with a beautiful mantle.

The first thing she had done when she walked in the door the evening before and saw the gorgeous mantle was to dig through her suitcases to find her favorite picture of her mom and herself. She remembered the day the picture was taken. She had been about six years of age at the time and the car that she and her mom had been driving in had broken down. Savannah had been a little apprehensive as she seemed to be an old soul and worried about everything. While they were waiting for Ted to come and pick them up, they heard the neighborhood ice cream truck going by. It had stopped and a long line had formed with kids anxiously wait-ing to spend their hard earned allowance. Sensing her little girl's fears, Savannah's mom had asked her if she would like to get an ice cream. She had hoped that the ice cream would get her mind off their latest little problem. Her mom had grabbed her hand and Savannah had looked up at her with a huge smile. Just then, Ted had pulled up and saw the pair. He had just come from a pho-tography class he was taking when he had received the desperate call from his friend and co-worker. When he saw the two cresting the grassy hill, he had picked up his camera and caught the happy moment on film. Ted had given the picture to her mom the fol-lowing Christmas and it had been proudly displayed in her mom's house.

Savannah wiped a tear from her cheek as she remembered

packing her mom's stuff and picking up the picture. Ted had been there too and had hugged her until her tears subsided. She smiled as she remembered how she felt walking away from that ice cream truck with her favorite ice cream, a Neapolitan ice cream sandwich, and her favorite person in the whole world, her mom. Then, she thought about Jim and how much her mom would have loved him.

With that comforting thought, she quickly got herself ready to set out and explore the surroundings of her new address.

CHAPTER
SIXTEEN

The rest of the day went by in a blur. She had found a bustling little coffee shop where she sat for a while observing the patrons and enjoying a tall mocha. Although the sun was out, there was still a chill in the air that left her cheeks rosy and her hands numb. She spoke to a woman who was ahead of her in line and told her that she was new to the area. The woman had welcomed her warmly and told her about a great antique store and a charming local art shop. She had also mentioned that at the end of the block there was a farmer's market that was inside during the winter months but still had all the fresh fruits and veggies for the season at reasonable prices. They also carried flowers and plants for the house.

After browsing the antique store, Savannah went in to the art shop and was taken aback by the colorful works of art. Everything you could possibly imagine was there and Savannah spent the rest of the morning and into early afternoon talking to the various artists about their pieces and discovered what had motivated them to create such inspirational works of art. She was fascinated by the colors in a beautiful glass pitcher and ended up buying it. Although it could be used for iced beverages, she knew she would not put it to use and instead display it on the little hutch that was in her kitchen. It was perfect.

She entered the farmer's market just as they were getting ready to close and bought some squash, potatoes and carrots. She had walked by a little corner grocery store on her way downtown and had decided to stop in and buy some meat for beef stew. As she gathered up her purchases from the farmer's market, she saw a beautiful purplish daisy plant, which she knew would look great in her new home and bought that as well.

As she stepped outside, her arms laden with her precious buys, she noticed dark clouds forming and wondered if she was going to be caught in a storm. She was no stranger to bad weather but didn't want to get her things wet. She slipped into the corner market just as the hovering dark cloud split in two. The market was small but had an appealing little fresh meat section where she waited in line to purchase her stew meat. As the man in front of her picked up his selected items he turned to face Savannah. She recognized him as the man who had offered to get her coffee when she was pitching her product at *The Ripe and Ready Fruit Company*.

"Savannah right?" He smiled. "Ron from the fruit company. Do you remember me? I was in the meeting when you came to present your product. I am the Controller at *The Ripe and Ready Fruit Company*."

His smile was genuine and Savannah instantly liked him. She had remembered him and how thoughtful he had been.

"Yes. Hi Ron."

A lively conversation ensued over the next few minutes. Savannah was careful not to mention Jim in the conversation, as she wanted to make sure she was abiding by the agreement that she and Jim had made.

Ron invited Savannah over for dinner that evening, saying that his wife would love to meet her and he suggested that it would be better than staying home alone in a strange new town. Savannah thought about the meat she was buying but decided to take Ron up on his offer. She could make the stew tomorrow and it would be ready when Jim came home that night. Ron said he would stop by and pick her up since she didn't have a vehicle. He mentioned that they didn't live too far away anyway.

He said he would come to pick her up around 6:30 p.m. Savannah was excited to have dinner with a new co-worker and looked forward to meeting his wife. She couldn't wait to tell Jim about it when he called.

Jim had been happy that she had made a friend and knew that Ron was a good guy. He mentioned that he also knew his wife and that they were nice people. The fact that Jim knew Ron and his wife so well made Savannah feel more comfortable and she was ready when Ron showed up promptly.

The rain had let up and, although there was a cool breeze, she left the house without a jacket. She had chosen to wear jeans and a green pullover sweater that hugged her figure and wasn't too bulky. She wore black boots with a small heel, comfortable but accomplished the task of making her feel a little taller then she actually was.

She had purchased a bottle of wine after she had left Ron and, when Ron's wife Jackie opened the door for them, Savannah handed the bottle to her with a smile. Jackie's face lit up with pleasure and welcomed her warmly into their home.

Jackie looked to be in her early 30's with shoulder length dirty blonde hair. She was tall, probably at least 5'7" and well proportioned. She and Ron made a great looking couple as he too appeared to be in his 30's probably closer to mid 30s and stood about six feet tall. He had light brown hair and they both had beautiful blue eyes.

Their house was small but filled with warmth and love. They had a two year old who came running out from another room to see who was attached to the voice he heard. Ryder was a brilliant mix of the handsome couple taking the olive skin tone of his dad and the blonde hair from his mom. He had turquoise eyes that sparkled with happiness.

Dinner was delicious. Jackie had made beef stroganoff with egg noodles and steamed vegetables. A Caesar salad and garlic bread were also part of the meal. Savannah learned that Ron and Jackie had met at work and Jackie had quit work when Ryder had been born. She and Ron had been married for four years and when Ryder had come along, they both couldn't have been happier. They opted to move out of their condo and move into a small house as they wanted to make sure that Jackie could stay home to raise their son. A bigger house would have meant that Ryder would have to go to daycare and they had both agreed that no home was worth that.

They laughed and talked all evening and at around 10:00 p.m., Savannah thought that she should probably get going. Ron got up to take her home and Savannah thanked Jackie for the lovely dinner. Earlier in the evening, Ron had put Ryder to bed and read him a bedtime story while Jackie and Savannah had done the dishes and cleaned the kitchen. They had connected immediately and had talked a mile a minute as if they had known each other for years.

Now, as they said their goodbyes, Jackie suggested that maybe they could get together and go shopping one afternoon.

As Savannah got in to Ron's car she was happy that she had made her first friends in Santa Barbara. She really liked, no *loved* it here!

Jim arrived at Savannah's place late Friday night. There had been a delay leaving Colorado, another bad winter snowstorm, and by the time he got to Savannah he was beat. Although she had a lot to tell him, she could tell he was really tired and opted to wait until Saturday morning when he was fresh. He left her place after a long hug and loving kiss and went home to his own house, still in the same complex but in a different wing. Because many employees lived in the complex, it was important that no one see Jim coming and going from Savannah's house.

Savannah slept soundly that night very happy with the direction her life had taken. It was a far cry from the depressing winter weather of Lancaster and the constant memories of Joel. She was shocked at how those painful memories still laid so close to the surface and was more than a little irritated about how those old wounds could tear open so quickly leaving her heart bleeding with emotional turmoil.

Savannah opened the door Saturday morning to Jim's smiling face. They were taking a chance, they both knew, but figured it would be ok for Jim to stop by and see if the new hire was settling in. She had cooked a nice breakfast for him and after breakfast and some very intimate reconnecting time, they spent the day driving around the town in a rental car that they had picked up. They did not want to drive around in a company car, as it would be a dead giveaway to any coworkers if they were seen together. Checking in on her was one thing. Spending the entire day together was yet another and they did not want to start any rumors. The rental car provided somewhat of a cover for them, at least for the time being, as no one would recognize the car or give it a second glance.

Ted and Bette arrived in Santa Barbara Sunday afternoon and both Jim and Savannah were there to greet them. They had decided it would be ok if the four of them were seen together as Jim could be the one helping the new employees get situated.

They ate dinner at a small restaurant that overlooked the ocean. Although it was winter, the waves had a peaceful way about them as they raced to shore. Ted and Bette were amazed at the beautiful weather for February. Neither of them had ever been to Santa Barbara and the smiles on their faces showed how pleased they were with their new surroundings.

It was cool out but the restaurant had a fireplace in the middle of the room and the tables were nestled in around it. There was soft music in the background that provided a cozy romantic feel. The candle-lit tables, linen tablecloths, and smell of warm fresh bread made this restaurant a magnet for both tourists and locals alike. Jim had made reservations Saturday morning, anticipating a possible crowd. The fire crackled behind the group as they talked about plans for first thing Monday morning. There was also the discussion about keeping Jim and Savannah's relationship a secret until the one-year merger was complete.

They had a great time laughing and talking, and enjoying each other's company. It made Savannah feel good that the people who mattered most in her life liked each other remembering the awkwardness of Ted and Joel's interactions.

After Jim and Savannah had dropped Ted and Bette off, Jim took Savannah home. A company employee would come to pick Savannah and Ted up the next day to begin their work at *The Ripe and Ready Fruit Company*. Savannah had the rental car that she would use the rest of the week, and then she was planning on purchasing a used car the following weekend. She and Jim talked about the fact that it was going to be difficult to keep their relationship a secret for a whole year but it would be exciting as well.

CHAPTER
SEVENTEEN

And what an exciting year it had been. Summer time came and while the days were filled with work, the evenings were spent talking to, and seeing Jim whenever he was in town, which was occurring more and more often these days. He had used the excuse of wanting to be around more to make sure the new "investment" was running smoothly. They had found a number of ways to slip around town unnoticed, and in the process had gotten to experience every hot spot Santa Barbara had to offer. Although they had wanted to spend time with Ron and Jackie, they were not officially able to. Instead they would plan chance meetings with Ron, Jackie and Savannah going out someplace only to run in to Jim who just happened to be at the place they were going. As Jim was conveniently by himself, Ron, being the great guy that he was, always invited Jim to join them somehow making the foursome ok.

The four of them had a great time as Jim and Ron had a long history of working together and they also had gone to high school together. They had known each other in high school but they hadn't hung out together as Ron was a couple years older and had been more into the business accounting classes while Jim had chosen the machine shop, woodshop type of electives. In his senior year of high school, Jim had gone to an off-site machine shop ROP class in order to help with the family business.

While Ron attended college, he applied to *The Ripe and Ready Fruit Company* as an Accountant. At Jim's recommendation, Jim's dad had hired him. His dad had been hesitant because he didn't have a degree but Jim was confident that he was a conscientious guy and a good worker. He told his dad that he felt Ron was trustworthy and he would vouch for him. Ron had excelled at his position and Jim's dad was pleased. By that time, Ron and Jim had started hanging out more and more, and had become good friends. Then Jackie came along and Ron was distracted. When Jim's parents had passed, within months of each other, Jim had a huge responsibility given to him and didn't have time to do much of anything but work for a long while. He lost track of all his old friends.

Jim's dad had gone first. He died in his sleep and the doctors had said he died of natural causes, whatever that meant. He was 75. His mother had died just a couple of months later, at 73, of a heart attack. She had been heart broken without her other half and Jim had suspected that it would only be a matter of time. It had happened sooner than he anticipated however, and had left him devastated. He had been very close to his parents and had thrown himself in to the business to keep their memory alive. Now with Savannah in his life and reconnecting with Ron and Jackie, Jim felt like his life was finally back on track.

Aside from sneaking around Santa Barbara, weekends were spent outside the city limits to allow Jim and Savannah to spend 48 hours of uninterrupted time together. Although they spent a lot of time in their hotel room, they did manage to get out and see what the various surrounding towns had to offer.

Savannah was amazed at how much she and Jim had in common. She was more amazed that she still felt so excited every time she saw him. They spent every weekend together and Friday nights were like Christmas Eve as the anticipated weekend approached. The ultimate "Christmas morning" was the connection on Saturday morning. She didn't see him too often during the week, as he was either out of town at other plants or just in a different area of the plant than where she worked.

His typical week was spent mostly at the Boulder plant, as it always had issues that needed to be dealt with. The Plant Manager, Bryce, was getting up in years and would soon be retiring. His energy level wasn't there and he was resistant to try anything new. Although Jim had helped him move the plant along, Jim was spending more and more time there just doing managerial things. He would never force Bryce to retire as Bryce had worked for the company since the beginning and, at one time, had been the right hand man to Jim's dad. In his younger days, he had implemented many procedures and had been a key player in making the company the successful one that it was today. Jim and Savannah had talked a little about him and they had both agreed that Bryce needed to retire on his own terms with his head held high. They knew the day was coming and Jim had made the decision that he would go there weekly, if needed, to make sure the plant continued to run successfully.

The plants in Minnesota and Alabama were much smaller and required minimal attention. They each had their specialty and seemed to run smoothly without too much management from Jim.

When Jim stayed in Santa Barbara for meetings with Carlie or to observe the ongoing production of the new product, Savannah took great pains to look her best. She wanted to make sure that, if she ran into Jim and he saw her, she would leave him with a lasting memory. Each time they did run in to each other the electrifying current was exhilarating. She wondered if anyone else in the room could feel it, and her face heated up just thinking about it.

Savannah spent a good chunk of time with Carlie as she was the main Project Manager for the new product and had a great deal of input as to how the blending of the companies was handled. Savannah had been impressed with Carlie's knowledge but noticed she seemed to be a little rough around the edges. She kept it in check quite convincingly but every once in a while, Carlie would say an off the cuff comment or over react to an issue that would leave Savannah questioning her.

Once, when they had been working late, Carlie had mentioned something about Jim and how she thought he hadn't made a good decision on some company issue that had come up. As she was explaining it to Savannah, her face had taken on a reddish hue and she looked like she was ready to burst. As Savannah saw her negative mood escalating she had asked Carlie why she was so angry. Carlie had quickly regained her composure and laughed it off, saying that Jim hadn't listened to her idea and that was his choice. "He is the Boss" she had said with a forced smile. The awkwardness of that moment, along with a few others, had left Savannah with an uncomfortable feeling. Carlie still did not know Savannah and Jim were a couple, and as the year went on, it became more important to Savannah that Carlie not be privy to that piece of information.

Savannah kept the odd feeling from Jim, as she knew Carlie was the right hand of the company and Jim depended on her and trusted her judgment. Their partnership had worked for them and together they had grown a very successful company and she wasn't about to stir up trouble.

She didn't share her feelings with Ted either as he was busy in another area of the company. She didn't see him as often as she used to. They tried to get together at least once ever other week for lunch but when they did, they both had so much to say that the couple of things Savannah had witnessed or the uneasy feeling that she was starting to get all too often, seemed unimportant.

Little did she know that Ted was struggling with his own observations.

CHAPTER EIGHTEEN

Ted loved working at the new company and really loved Santa Barbara. He was busy in the processing department making sure that the swivel arm on the new fruit processor turned just right. They seemed to be having a problem getting the arm to the exact angle and had to keep readjusting the cut of the material. Rick, the engineer that had been working on the prototype in Santa Barbara, could not get the swivel right and would not listen to any suggestions that Ted had. He kept saying that *he* was the Engineer and *he* knew what he was doing. Up until now, he hadn't and they were running out of time, as the plan was to unveil the finished product at the agricultural convention in late March.

The agricultural convention was a chance for all the farmers in California to meet and share ideas about growing, processing and selling all fruits and vegetables. If they wanted to get any new product into the market, that convention was the time to unveil it.

Both Ted and Carlie knew it would be a huge success but timing was everything and if they couldn't get this swivel arm to work, they would miss this all-important deadline.

Ted was concerned, as he knew the final sign off on the company sale would be the prototype of the finished product. They had made several small variations at his company in Lancaster and he *knew* that the product was real, could be built and worked. He couldn't understand why it wasn't working here. He also didn't understand why Rick wouldn't listen to him. It was frustrating and he was losing patience.

He had kept in contact with everyone from the old company in Lancaster, and he and Bob, the engineer from his plant, had remained good friends. Bob had been hired as the head engineer over at the Lancaster *Ripe and Ready* plant and had brought a wealth of knowledge with him. Bob and Ted still shared stories about the old company and the good times they had experienced. Bob had mentioned that things were very different at the new plant and sometimes he questioned how things were done. When he had mentioned it to Ted he then said that he was probably just so accustomed to the well-run company that Ted had created. The way this company was run just seemed unorthodox.

Ted had laughed it off and had asked for Bob's advice on the swivel arm and how the problem could be solved. After listening to Bob's ideas, Ted asked Bob if he would be willing to fly to Santa Barbara to work with Rick, the engineer. Ted mentioned he would have to run it by Carlie but he felt if the two of them could work together, they could get over this hump and get the product finished.

It was already late October and Ted was getting really worried. He thought again about the proposition he had made to Bob and decided to approach Carlie. He had a meeting with her late one Thursday afternoon. It was the day before Halloween and staff seemed to be distracted by the upcoming Halloween festivities that were due to take place the next day. Because Halloween fell on Friday this year, they had decided to have everyone dress up for work and have a company Halloween party that would go into the evening. Various staff members were hanging blinking lights

and spreading spider web material over the corners of the conference room. Everyone was in a jovial mood and shouting back and
forth about other ideas for making the most amazing decorations
ever.

Carlie and Ted ended up in Carlie's office with the door closed
to try to get a bit of quiet time. Ted explained the situation they
were running into down in the production room with the non-
swiveling arm. He also mentioned that although he and Rick had
tried many different things, they were not able to make it work.
He was careful not to mention the fact that Rick was impossible
to work with and wouldn't listen to any of Ted's suggestions. He
didn't want to be disrespectful to anyone as that wasn't his nature.
Ted did mention though, that Rick had his own way of doing
things. He stopped short of saying that he didn't know *what* he
was doing.

Carlie seemed to become uneasy instantly. She defended Rick
even though nothing had been said to warrant a defense. Ted
looked at Carlie then *really* looked at her and, slowly the wheels
began to turn. He put two and two together and realized, with a
sick knot in his stomach, that Carlie had a thing for Rick. As he
thought back on it now, it made perfect sense.

Ted had noticed that whenever Carlie had come out to the
production floor to check on the production, she had had a smile
on her face and a twinkle in her eye. Carlie appeared to be in her
early 40s and was pleasant to look at. Not striking by any means,
just decent. She had short brown hair and brown eyes. She stood
about 5'7" and dressed very professionally. She was evenly proportioned and seemed to have an air about her that demanded
respect. That "air" however, broke down when Rick was around.
Rick was much older than Carlie, maybe 10 years her senior, with
a rough exterior. His hair was salt and pepper with salt getting
more of the stage .He was tall, about 6'3", but much more on the
casual side wearing jeans most days. He was a Senior Engineer
and for that reason was treated with respect among others in the

production area. While Carlie commanded respect with her pres-
ence, Rick commanded respect with his mouth. He was quick to
remind everyone of who he was and what his title was. He was
a nice guy, just not at work. He was arrogant and obnoxious at
work, but Carlie didn't seem to notice.

So, while Carlie was busy defending Rick, Ted just listened
quietly and fully understood. When she was done, Ted turned
things around. He had thought about it quickly and realized that
he was going to have to broach this subject very discreetly or she
would definitely turn it down. Love was a funny thing.

So, he reminded Carlie about how the deadline was fast
approaching and said he had a great suggestion that might get
the product moving. Without mentioning Rick's name, Ted suggested that she should fly Bob out for a week to see if he could
help out in production. Then he stated with a smile, that two engi-
neers were better than one.

With that, he gave her the opportunity to think about it and
stood up to leave making some excuse that he had to get home to
Bette. He also put a spin on the idea saying that Carlie had probably thought of the idea already. She nodded and said, "Well I was
thinking of bringing someone in to help but I hadn't thought of
Bob. Let me think about it and I will let you know."

Ted smiled as he left her office. The seed had been planted.

CHAPTER
NINETEEN

Ted waited for Bob's plane to land smiling with the realization that his plan had worked. Carlie had come in to his office first thing Monday morning asking him to make arrangements to have Bob fly out to help with the production problem. Ted had not missed a beat and now, one week later, Bob was on his way. The squealing sound of the baggage wheel in the distance reminded him of the Halloween party he had experienced at *The Ripe and Ready Fruit Company*. It had been quite an event to say the least! Much different than any company party he had experienced before.

Staff had gone all out with decorations and food, and the costumes were amazing. Everyone participated in dressing up and it was interesting to get to know people outside of the traditional work environment. They played games, had a costume contest and even had a piñata. The twist to the piñata was that the "candy" pieces inside were instead small envelopes containing puzzle pieces, which came in all shapes and sizes. When someone acquired an envelope they would put the puzzle together and take it to the "gift" area to redeem the prize that the completed puzzle revealed. Winners received gift cards to various local coffee houses and restaurants. The grand prize was a wad of cash totaling $500.00. The puzzle for that prize was a picture of a fat roll of paper money. Once the piñata broke, everyone scurried to grab an envelope. Apparently, this was a company tradition as everyone rushed over to the piñata like a group of kids. Their coworkers tried to fill in Savannah, Ted and Bette while keeping a close eye on the piñata in case it suddenly burst. It was great fun and everyone had walked away from the game with a smile and a nice gift.

Ted and Bette sat at a table with Savannah and Ted was happy that he had been able to spend more time with her. Because Ted was around Savannah, it was a little more convenient for Jim to be around too. Ron and Jackie had completed the table of six where they sat to eat the ghoulish meal that had been catered for the event.

The company had spared no expense and Ted and Savannah had each commented that it was the best Halloween party they had ever attended. Because no one had talked about work, Ted had not had the opportunity to tell Savannah that Bob was coming to town. He knew that Savannah would be very excited to hear about Bob's arrival but knew she would start questioning why he was there. She would probably ask why the engineer on staff wasn't able to complete the task at hand. After all, there was a very detailed manual that had been especially written to be able to create the device. It had been years in the making and was very precise.

Come to think of it, Ted also wondered why Rick was not able to read the manual and follow the procedures. Ted began piecing the facts together but was interrupted by a familiar voice that jerked him back to reality.

Bob's plane had landed and now Bob was walking over to him calling his name with a big grin on his face. He was full of energy as he took in the bright winter skies of California. He had just left

Lancaster in the midst of another storm and felt energized by the west coast sun.

Ted took Bob to a little cafe near the office where they ate a hearty breakfast and discussed the afternoon meeting with Rick. Ted explained the difficult personality that Bob would have to deal with and also shared an observation he had witnessed regarding a possible relationship between Carlie and Rick. He provided this assessment to Bob for protection as he knew that Carlie had clout in all of the company plants and he wanted to make sure Bob didn't do or say anything to jeopardize his job back home.

Bob thanked him, and the remainder of the meal was nice. Bob asked how Savannah was doing and Ted almost spilled the beans about Jim and her. When Bob asked if she was seeing anyone it quickly reminded Ted of the position Bob held in the chess game of Savannah's life. He continued with the story line that had begun almost a year earlier stating that Savannah had thrown herself into her new job and had been very busy the past year. Bob accepted the story and said he was looking forward to seeing her. Ted also mentioned that he hadn't shared the whole "Rick" situation with Savannah and would prefer not to worry her just yet. As they were both very protective of her, the suggestion made sense to Bob and an agreement was made. They both knew that Savannah worried a lot and they didn't want to stir something up that might be nothing. Ted silently reasoned that Bob did not know that Savannah had a direct line to the head guy and he wanted to make sure that everything was completed on this merger without any feathers ruffled.

As it turned out, after the meeting, Savannah ran into Bob coming out of the production conference room. She had gone down there to take a couple of pictures and gather information for the brochures that she and her staff were busy creating. She was happy, surprised and confused as she embraced Bob with a generous hug. Ted came out a moment later and stood back to let the reunion take place. Before questions could start being asked, Ted suggested that they meet for dinner. Just then Rick appeared suggesting that a group dinner might be nice. Awkwardly Ted agreed and Rick suggested that Carlie and Jim, if he was in town, also join the group. Ted realized what was going on. Rick wanted to make sure there would be no "closed door meetings" that might reveal the ability (or in Rick's case lack of ability) that seemed to be causing the production delay.

As it turned out, Jim was in town and it was decided that they would meet at a local restaurant for dinner and drinks. Savannah was excited as she hadn't seen Jim since Halloween and was looking forward to spending some time with him regardless of the distance they would have to keep. This past weekend had been only the second weekend they had been apart in the last year and she was amazed at how much he had become a part of her life. And the shocker was she had let him in. Against everything that she had promised herself!

Bette couldn't join the group for dinner so it was just the six of them. Savannah had rushed back to her place to freshen up and redo her make up and hair. She wore a red fitted sweater that stopped midway down her hips and a pair of black jeans tucked into ankle boots. A thin white scarf with red flecks and silver hoop earrings finished the look. Her hair was parted on the side and gently curled framing her face. She looked at the mirror and smiled at what stared back. She felt radiantly happy.

As she walked into the restaurant she noticed Jim, Carlie and Rick had already arrived. Jim stood up immediately when he saw her and the all-to-familiar magnetic pull reached out to hypnotize her as their eyes met and locked. Once again she lost all her senses and, with a flushed face, walked straight over to him. She didn't hear the door open immediately behind her, and when Ted called her name out, it broke the trance she and Jim seemed to be in, just in the nick of time. There cover was not blown but it was too close for comfort in Ted's opinion as he now felt that Carlie knowing about their relationship would be disastrous.

Dinner conversation was light and with the wine flowing freely, the group talked and laughed the evening away. Ted, however, was quiet as he assessed the group. He noticed Jim and Savannah staring at each other – they seemed to be flirting with nothing more than their eyes but it felt like they were screaming, "look at us" to Ted. Then there was Carlie and Rick. He wasn't sure what was going on there but he knew the chemistry on that side of the table was boiling over as well. Bob seemed oblivious to the whole thing and Ted was happy when Bob mentioned that he wanted to call it a day and head back to the hotel. After all, he had been up for many more hours than everyone else and suddenly was experiencing jet lag.

As everyone said their goodbyes, Ted chuckled to himself. *Rick is a sneaky man*, Ted thought. *He managed to have everyone together and not mention anything about work.* Ted realized then that he was dealing with a very deceptive individual. He didn't know how to prove it and that was the problem. He made a vow to figure out how to expose the person who was making his life miserable. He would make it happen, he just didn't know how quite yet.

CHAPTER TWENTY

The holidays were a whirlwind. Thanksgiving came and Savannah was surprised at the minimal change in weather. Back in Lancaster they would be freezing about now and possibly even experiencing a little bit of snow.

Savannah and Jim had spent Thanksgiving with Ted and Bette and had then taken off to Palm Springs for the rest of the weekend. The days were spent sightseeing and shopping. The nights were spent wrapped in each other's arms exploring all there was to know about each other and discovering happiness over and over again.

Back at work, things were starting to move quickly. Bob had worked with Rick and taught him what needed to get done to get the arm to swivel at precisely the angle that was needed. Bob had a way with people and was able to get through to Rick and get him to listen. Ted had chalked it up to "engineer talk" as he had tried to explain the same idea to Rick but it had fallen on deaf ears.

By Christmas, the product was done just in time for the Christmas/New Year plant shut down. As everyone was saying their goodbyes until January, Ted, Savannah, Rick and Carlie were tying up some loose ends.

When they returned after the holidays, there would be a few last minute details, and by mid February the sale would be finalized and the merger would be completed. Carlie had asked both Ted and Savannah if they would like to remain on as permanent employees. Jim, in his ever-professional manner, had not mentioned a word to Savannah and she was very happy with the employment offer. Ted and Bette had also discussed an extended stay and decided to go for it. Although their kids were back east, they were busy with their lives and promised to come and visit in the spring. The timing had been perfect because Savannah had been looking at possibly putting a down payment on a beautiful townhome she had visited during an open house. She and Jim had celebrated Jim's 32nd birthday the first week in December and then he had left for Boulder. Savannah and Jackie had gone Christmas shopping one day and came across the "Open House" sign for a new townhome development across the street from the beach. Upon going inside, Savannah loved everything about it and was seriously thinking about making an offer on the unit that had a view of the ocean. The job offer made her decision an easy one. There was only one left and she really wanted to show Jim and Ted the place before she made a big purchase like that.

By the time either of them was available to go look at the place, it was gone. Someone had purchased it right out from under her. She was disappointed at first but Ted said that everything happens for a reason. She agreed with that kind of thinking and knew that something else would come along. In the meantime, effective March 1st, she would continue to live in the condo that *The Ripe and Ready Fruit Company* had provided for her and pay rent to the company. Ted and Bette decided to do the same.

It will do for now, Savannah thought, but dreamed of owning a small house on the beach. She could picture it now – a cozy little house close to the beach with a view of waves rushing to the shore. And Jim. *Perfect,* she thought and smiled.

CHAPTER
TWENTY-ONE

Savannah woke up on February 1st and flipped the calendar. She realized that she had only spoken to Trish a few times in the past year and wondered how married life was treating her. She realized that it had already been almost a year since she had seen her best friend and decided that a trip to Lancaster was long over due.

Savannah was scheduled to start her new position as Marketing Director in March and she would be instrumental in presenting the new product at the upcoming agricultural convention. She had worked hard to get all the documentation on the product assembled and had put together beautiful color brochures. There had been several prototypes made to display in several different colors and sizes. They had decided which fruits and vegetables they were going to use to demonstrate the new product and everything seemed to be in place.

She talked to Jim that evening and told him of her plans. She had spoken to Trish earlier and she was excited to have Savannah come for a visit. She immediately started planning things for them to do and told her to bring warm clothes because Lancaster was experiencing a cold spell that was off the charts.

Jim was happy that Savannah was getting the opportunity to see her old friend and explained that he was not able to go due to several issues at the Colorado plant. Savannah was disappointed but understood. He promised that he would be back in Santa Barbara before Valentine's Day and had planned to take her somewhere special for the weekend.

She left early Thursday morning and was lucky enough to have Ted drop her off at the airport. She boarded the plane with excitement as she was looking forward to seeing her old stomping grounds.

The flight was turbulent and she was exhausted and relieved when the plane finally touched down at the Lancaster airport. Trish was waiting for her outside the baggage claim area and when they saw each other, they ran to each other and hugged like it had been years.

Trish hadn't changed much except for a shorter hairstyle that made her features even more appealing. She was a striking woman and married life apparently agreed with her. She was radiant in her winter white coat and blue jeans.

Their first stop was to their favorite coffee shop to get warmed up and reminisce about old times. They would both be celebrating their 30th birthdays in March and had commented that last March had been the first time since they met that they hadn't celebrated their special day together. They decided to make one night of Savannah's visit their birthday celebration night. After spending a long time at the coffee shop, they finally headed back to Trish's house.

Bill and Trish had purchased a cute little house in the older part of town and were working together to remodel it. So far, the kitchen and one bathroom had been remodeled as well as a beautiful backyard deck, which, at the moment, was covered by a thin layer of snow.

Savannah was suddenly very tired and longed for a quick nap. Trish ushered her to a small room that was decorated with a southern flare. The room had various pictures of the countryside with green rolling hills and fields of yellow flowers.

The queen-sized bed was dressed in a beautiful white and green comforter. The bed had a white chiffon canopy that draped across the top with the ends cascading down the corners of the bed. The throw pillows were a mixture of various shades of green that made the room feel bright but cozy. The down pillows beckoned her, and with that she lay on the bed as she listened to Trish talk a mile a minute. Savannah was so exhausted from the stressful plane trip that she couldn't keep her eyes open any longer. As she was drifting off to sleep, Savannah heard Trish say "we have big plans for tonight so get all rested up." Savannah was out.

Savannah woke up late in the afternoon, close to 5:00 p.m. The winter sun was almost down and when Savannah entered the dimly lit living room, Trish jumped as she seemed preoccupied and Savannah had startled her. Then she smiled from ear to ear. She pushed Savannah to hurry up and get ready and to wear something nice as they were going to a new little French restaurant that has just opened in town. She said that she and Bill had been waiting for a special occasion to eat there and Savannah being in town marked that event. Savannah smiled.

"We can celebrate our birthdays," she said. With that she told Savannah to go get ready. Trish had made reservations for 7:00 p.m. Bill had to work late and was going to meet them there. Savannah decided to wear a dress she had picked up right before her trip to Lancaster. It was a black and royal blue pencil dress that rested about two inches above her knees. The sleeves were three-quarter length, which allowed her to show off the beautiful bracelet Jim had given her for Christmas. A black belt that cinched her waist complimented the outfit perfectly. She chose to wear black tights and boots that would help to keep her warm.

When she entered the living room, Trish complimented her on how amazing she looked. Trish was dressed in a forest green sweater dress with a black belt and a short black jacket. The two were quite a beautiful pair as they walked in to the restaurant. It had just started snowing outside which made the restaurant more warm and inviting.

As the door closed behind them, Trish looked down and said she had left her phone in the car and wanted to get it in case Bill tried to call. She asked Savannah to tell them they had a reservation and that she would be right back. She said, "I am so excited to go to this place. Everyone has been talking about it and it is very hard to get a table."

Trish's excitement was contagious and Savannah obediently went to the desk to get the table that had been reserved for them. She watched as Trish scurried back out into the weather noting how beautiful the snowflakes looked falling gently out of the sky. The entry hall was warm and inviting and a young hostess not more than 20 years old smiled, waiting to greet arriving customers.

Savannah said that she had a reservation and gave Trish's name. The smile quickly left the girl's face as she realized there was no reservation under that name. Savannah looked past her and saw that the small dining room was completely filled.

"There must be some mistake," she said. "My friend made this reservation a few days ago and called today to confirm it." The young girl's face looked devastated as she combed the reservation list yet another time. Savannah knew Trish would be so disapointed if they didn't eat at this wonderful place. "What about under Savannah?" she asked. "Is there a reservation under the name Savannah?"

The girl looked down the list and blushed as she found her name and smiled widely. "Yes," she said. "Come right this way." A wave of relieve flooded over Savannah, as she knew Trish would have been heartbroken if they would not have been able to get in.

The girl weaved her through the various clusters of tables and walked towards the back of the restaurant. *Oh,* Savannah thought. *There must be a whole other section in the back. This restaurant must be great.*

She turned the corner and stopped. The room was dimly lit with twinkling lights cascading the ceiling creating a romantic setting. There were only a few tables in the room and all were decorated with beautiful glowing candle centerpieces. The candlelight created shadows which danced around the walls and it took a minute for Savannah's eyes to adjust to the low lighting. Her eyes scanned the room taking a panoramic shot of the exquisite decorations and then she saw Jim. She was confused for a second and he stepped in to the light.

He was standing in front of her, just for a second, and then was down on one knee. He looked up at Savannah and said, "Savannah, will you spend the rest of your life with me and be my bride?" He held a small brown case in one hand and opened it up to display a beautiful diamond ring.

Savannah gasped as she took a deep breath. It took her a minute to process what was happening and to regain her composure. She looked down at his beautiful eyes and whispered, "Yes". He jumped up and put the ring on her finger. Then he hugged her and kissed her like he never had before. She was laughing and tears were streaming down her face.

Just then the door burst open and Trish and Bill came running over. Trish and Savannah hugged each other and squeals of excitement were exchanged. Bill and Jim shook hands then hugged each other to share their happiness.

They were seated at a table and enjoyed a bottle of the best champagne to celebrate the occasion. Savannah was so taken aback by the series of events that had just occurred that she was a little on the quiet side as she took in the ambiance of the room and tried to take a mental picture of the most perfect evening of her life. It took her a while to acknowledge that she was going to marry the man she was so in love with. She wished she could tell her mom. Tears instantly welled in her eyes as she thought about how much she missed her and wished she were there. She shook off the melancholy feelings and came back to the present – and this perfect moment.

The rest of the evening was spent enjoying their dinner and talking about when and where they were going to be married. Jim kept looking at Savannah and smiling and finally reached over to take her hand. The chemistry between them was so strong that the simple touch of his hand sent electricity through her body. Her face heated up and she had to look away to try to regain her composure. Jim chuckled under his breath and winked at her when she looked up. She smiled back and looked at Trish who had taken the whole scene in and smiled. She loved seeing her friend happy and in love at last.

After dinner they walked downtown as Savannah had wanted to share this special moment with the area where she grew up. The town had changed very little and was still beautiful. As the snow started to fall a little faster, they cut their walk short to get in out of the cold.

They quickly drove back to Trish and Bill's house before the weather got too bad to drive. Trish and Savannah drove in one car and Jim went with Bill. Savannah told Trish the whole story about not having a table under Trish's name and that Savannah, on a whim, had given the young hostess her own name. They laughed and as both cars pulled up to the house, Savannah felt like the luckiest woman in the world.

She thought, *my life has changed so much in the last two years I would have never predicted this.* And now, she thought her life was complete.

She had no idea what was in store for her in the not-too-distant future.

CHAPTER TWENTY-TWO

The rest of the weekend was wonderful and went by quickly. Savannah was so glad that Jim had been able to get away for the weekend and she suddenly felt like everything was different. She felt so connected to him and she truly couldn't imagine her life without him.

Savannah, Trish and Bill had taken Jim around to a couple of their favorite hang outs and they all laughed and reminisced about what life had been like growing up in Lancaster. They also did a lot of eating and talking about the upcoming wedding. They also managed to go out for Savannah and Trish's "birthday celebration" and chose a little comedy club in town. The comedian had heard that the two were celebrating their 30th birthdays and he ribbed them relentlessly. The whole place was laughing and Trish and Savannah had to go up and take a bow at the end of the evening. Jim snapped a picture of them laughing and sent it to everyone's cell phones. A great memory was now preserved for a lifetime.

When Bill and Trish dropped Jim and Savannah off at the airport Sunday afternoon, Trish and Savannah made a vow to try to get together much more often. Savannah told Trish that she would let her know the wedding date the moment it was decided, as Trish would be her Matron of Honor.

They exchanged long hugs and Jim and Savannah proceeded to the security line that awaited them. Although they were taking separate flights (Jim had to go back to Colorado and Savannah was going to Santa Barbara) their flights didn't leave for another hour and a half so they could sit and talk about everything that had happened during the weekend and the wonderful life plans that were in store for them. They also had to decide when they were going to go public with their relationship.

Ted was picking Savannah up at the Santa Barbara airport. She couldn't wait to tell him the news and show him her beautiful ring. She looked down at her ring and looked up to see Jim smiling at her. She blushed and he leaned over and kissed her gently.

They talked about a possible date for their wedding and what kind of ceremony they wanted to have. The purchase of the company would be complete on February 15th. Then there was the big agricultural convention in March. They pondered whether or not to tell the employees before the convention and decided that the smarter thing to do was to wait until the convention was over. Everyone was so busy wrapping up last minute details they didn't want to do anything to break the momentum. They agreed on a September wedding, which would allow Savannah time to plan. Although she wanted just a small celebration, she wanted it to be special. She thought about what she had always imagined her wedding day would be like and realized that she hadn't really ever imagined getting married. In her young adult life she had been hurt so badly by Joel that she never entertained the idea of marriage. Now, sitting at the airport with the man of her dreams, she couldn't believe that she was finally able to allow herself to think about a wedding. Her wedding!

They went over the list of invitees and both realized that they didn't really have any family.

"Well," Jim said, "My Aunt will be the only blood relative of either one of us."

Savannah laughed and said, "When am I going to get a chance to meet her? I haven't heard you talk too much about her. Does she still live in Colorado?"

Jim looked at her with a stunned look. Then he said, "What...what do you mean? You already have met her."

Now it was Savannah's turned to look surprised.

"I have?" She questioned. "When did I meet her? What is her name?"

"Carlie. Carlie is my Aunt! I thought you knew that!"

Savannah's jaw dropped.

CHAPTER
TWENTY-THREE

"What?" Savannah echoed again. "Carlie is your Aunt? You've never mentioned that to me before."

Jim then went on to say that Carlie, Jim's dad's much younger sister, had left the Colorado area when Jim was six years old. At 18, Carlie was a headstrong young woman who wanted to see the world and get away from the family and spread her wings. She had traveled the world and had married an Italian man in Tuscany. She had lived there with him for many years until he was killed in a freak accident. By that time Jim was just about 20 and already heavily consumed with working in the family business. Carlie came home to regroup and had taken a menial job in town until Jim's dad hired her to manage the sales for the jelly product that the company was just beginning to sell. Carlie had done well and had some ideas that, once implemented, took the company in a successful direction. Carlie had found her niche and although she was heartbroken at the loss of her husband, she seemed happy and content. Jim had also been busy at the company and learned everything there was to know. Jim's parents were impressed at the way he had taken it upon himself to get educated in all things related to fruits and vegetables, and he was quite the people person as well. When Jim's parents passed and the business had been left to Jim, Carlie was more than a little upset as she had put the last six years of her life in to the company and had felt that the company should have been left to both Jim and herself.

When Jim moved the company in yet another business direction to include the environmental spin, Carlie had been taken aback and there had been conflict between the two. Carlie had felt they didn't need to expand any further and thought that the new leg of the company would jeopardize their current successful business. In fact just the opposite had occurred and the company had grown very successfully and had exploded in sales in every division including fresh fruits and vegetables, jams and jellies, canned fruits and now the environmental portion that processed expired fruits and vegetables, turning them into cleaning solutions and such.

After the initial conflict, Jim chose to never get into another power struggle with his aunt again and had decided to let her do what she did best, manage projects, while he oversaw the bigger picture and continued to move the company in the direction he felt strongly about: an environmentally sound company that used every fruit and vegetable to its fullest.

Although a few of the higher-level employees knew of the connection between Jim and Carlie, the majority did not and it had never been an issue. Carlie's Italian last name had been the cloak that covered the lineal heritage.

Savannah and Jim said their goodbyes shortly after the revelation had been shared, and Savannah walked toward her gate with a million questions swimming around her head. Did Ted know about this? Were Carlie and Jim close? Is that what Carlie had been alluding to when she had said Jim hadn't listened to her awhile back? Is that why Jim had wanted to keep their relationship quiet? She stopped short with the last question, as this was one she could answer. *She* had been the one that wanted to keep things quiet. She hadn't wanted any conflict between herself and the project manager who she now knew was Jim's aunt. She wondered if she had a sixth sense. She couldn't wait to discuss it with Jim that night. She was going to get the answers to all these questions.

CHAPTER TWENTY-FOUR

Jim had a busy afternoon. The Colorado branch had been work-ing on blending a couple of different variations of fruit to create a new flavor. It would be "all natural" and could be used as syrup, jelly or as an added ingredient in a favorite recipe. It hadn't been perfected yet but they were getting close and Jim was optimistic. It was going to be another product he planned to showcase at the convention.

As he looked out the taxicab window on his way home from the airport, he saw a young woman trying to maneuver her rolling luggage piece while limping along on crutches. She looked tired and beat and Jim immediately thought of Savannah and the night at the hotel when she had opened the door to her hotel room thinking it was room service. He chuckled as he remembered the surprised look on her face before she turned beat red. If he hadn't already been under her spell, that moment did the trick. He was captivated by her every move and knew right then, that he was falling in love. It just took her some time to realize they were meant for each other. His thoughts moved ahead to their most recent conversation at the airport. He couldn't believe that she didn't know that he and Carlie were related. He thought he had mentioned it that first night but, as he thought more about it, he realized he probably hadn't since he neglected to mention who *he* was that first night either. He had thought Savannah didn't want Carlie to know about them because she wanted to feel that she got the deal on her own and not because of him. Which was a true statement. *Well,* he thought. *I am sure it will all be ironed out tonight.* He smiled as he thought about skyping with Savannah that evening. He loved talking to her and seeing her face was a bonus. He was the luckiest man alive.

<center>~~~~~</center>

Ted and Bette picked Savannah up from the airport. Savannah was so excited to tell them the news and show them her beautiful engagement ring that she forgot all about the Carlie issue. Besides, she would talk to Jim first and get the back-story before she talked to anyone else.

Bette was ecstatic when she heard the news and looked forward to helping plan the special event. Ted was happy too and silently wished that Savannah's mother was still alive to see how radiant and successful her daughter was.

Ted dropped Savannah off at her door, and he and Bette drove down and around the complex to park near their own home. Bette had seemed to come to life now that she had a task to accomplish, planning Savannah's wedding. He was happy for her but was dealing with his own turmoil of this company they were involved in.

Ted had received more unsettling news and was trying to figure out exactly what was going on. He didn't have any concrete evidence but something wasn't right. He just didn't know what it was. First there was the strange situation with Rick the engineer. Then, Bob had said things were, what was the word he used to describe it at the Lancaster plant, unorthodox? Finally, Ron, the controller, had made an off the cuff comment that had set off alarms in Ted's head. Ron had actually been talking to Savannah when Ted just happened to overhear and see the look of uneasiness Ron's face wore. Now, with the unveiling of the new product just a few weeks away, he was feeling more ill at ease with every passing day but at least for now, he had to sit tight. With Valentine's Day fast approaching and the sale of the company complete on the 15th, Ted realized there was nothing he could do at the moment.

On Valentine's Day every year, *The Ripe and Ready Fruit Company* provided chocolate covered strawberries and fruit baskets to the senior care homes and the homeless shelters. They also donated mini fruit baskets to the non-profit organizations that provided grocery baskets to those in need. They had been doing this community service project for years and it took the entire week to prepare and make the deliveries. A noble effort was put forth by everyone and well worth it. Ted was caught up in the rush of it all and the good feeling that came with doing the right thing and for a short time, forgot the havoc that was brewing behind the scenes at *The Ripe and Ready Fruit Company.*

CHAPTER
TWENTY-FIVE

Roses were delivered bright and early to Savannah's desk on the 14th with a note from her mysterious secret admirer:

An air trip of destiny
A dream come true
My heart is complete
For now I have you

Happy Valentine's Day to the woman of my dreams
And a lifetime of happiness
And all that it brings

Love S.A.M.

Savannah smiled. SAM had become their code name and even Ted knew that SAM stood for Secret Admirer and was Jim's code name. Jim had put the initials S.A.M. on notes and cards he had given her early on when they had first started working together at the company. The very first note he had signed S.A(me) in parentheses. The acronym "SAM" had just stuck.

All her coworkers wanted to meet "Sam" and Savannah had promised that one day she would introduce him to the group. Everyone accepted that and they all agreed that he seemed like a wonderful guy. Savannah could not agree more. She thought back on their face time discussion the weekend before and the flurry of questions she had asked him about Carlie. He had answered them all and apologized for not being more clear with her. He had said that he and his aunt were not very close on a personal level but were good collaborators in the work force. He saw her enough and kept things for the most part, on a professional level. They really didn't have too much in common personally and there were no other relatives to bring them together on a family level. That explained why it had probably slipped his mind to tell Savannah. He did say that he didn't think Ted knew either unless Carlie had mentioned it to him, which he was skeptical about. Like Savannah, Carlie didn't want anyone thinking that she was in her position for any reason other than she had worked hard and earned it.

~~~~

"POP"! Corks flew off several bottles of champagne as the celebration of the completed merger took place. It was Friday afternoon, Valentines week had been successful, all prototypes were made and worked, and the merger was complete.

Although Savannah was now financially set for life, she didn't care too much about the money. She was more excited about finding happiness. And that she had.

CHAPTER
TWENTY-SIX

The week before the agricultural convention was crazy. All hands were on deck as they were preparing the final touches on the new device they had named "The Cutting Edge." Three different sizes were made and ready to go. The largest, in chrome, was for commercial use while the other two were for home use and single use. They had chosen to make one in red and one in yellow but would have brochures showing all the colors available including black, white and green. The commercial unit was quite large, about the size of a portable refrigerator in height but quite compact in width spanning only about 20" wide. The depth was also about 20", which made the piece of equipment fairly portable for movement within a company. The smaller "home" units were the size of a blender and could easily be dismantled for cleaning in the dishwasher.

They chose avocados, kumquats and oranges to showcase how the device could peel thick or thin-skinned fruit as well as peel and cut around a seed. The trick for cutting was to adjust the inner swivel arm, which was why they had had to get it just right. There was a special blade that could be attached to allow for the seed expulsion without cutting the fruit up. It helped to make for a cleaner cut and made dicing the fruit a breeze. There were other gadget attachments as well, but staff anticipated that they would be used more for commercial than home use. The additional attachments would allow fruit to be cut up in various shapes, more for show really, and would allow the cutting, peeling, and chopping work for large quantities of fruits and vegetables to occur in record time.

Although there would be a formal unveiling at the convention, Savannah and her team had performed some preliminary marketing feelers and were getting lots of interest and had heard only positive feedback. They already had three commercial orders in the works. The residential sales would come as a result of large companies buying the smaller version of the product and then reselling it to their customers. Everyone had done a good job and they were ready to fly to northern California where the convention was to be held.

The convention was a success and the entire weekend was spent demonstrating and networking. It had been held at a fairground just south of Silicon Valley and targeted farmers, restaurant owners and other manufacturing plants throughout California. The convention included various products, tools and other business related information that anyone in the food industry including restaurant owners and farmers could benefit from. Vendors had been set up all with the hopes of selling the newest and greatest of all things related to food. The weekend attendance was over five thousand which equaled a huge success for everyone involved. Although Jim, Carlie, Ted and Savannah were all there, they were spread out in different areas to allow exposure in each section of the huge convention hall. The weekend flew by. Their new Cutting Edge product had been well received and visitors had returned throughout the weekend to purchase the product. The end of the weekend had culminated with orders beyond their wildest dreams.

Everyone cheered and Ted was exceptionally proud, as he knew the original idea had been his. He had no regrets about the sale of the patent because he was wealthier then he could have ever imagined and there would have been no way he or his company in Lancaster could have produced the volume of orders that now had to be filled. He was excited to be part of it but very happy not to have the responsibility that came with the large number of orders they had collected.

The flight back to Santa Barbara was quick and before long everyone was home and anxious to get back to work. Jim came over to Savannah's that night no longer worried if anyone saw them together and brought Thai food and a bottle of wine. There was so much to celebrate.

After talking about work for a while and all the funny things that had happened at the convention, the conversation turned more intimate. Before long they had moved to a more comfortable setting to explore each other intimately. When they finally drifted off to sleep, they were content on every level.

CHAPTER
TWENTY-SEVEN

Although Monday morning came quickly, they were in no rush to get going. The wrap up meeting was scheduled for after lunch and everyone was expected to be in the office by the 1:00 p.m. meeting time.

Jim and Savannah had decided they were going to tell the staff members about their relationship and engagement at the end of the meeting. They couldn't think of any reason not to, now that the sale of the company was complete and the money had officially changed hands. The convention had been successful and was now behind them. The timing was perfect.

The meeting was held in the same conference room where Savannah had given her original presentation. The room was full, with every manager and division head seated and ready to hear the results of the convention and the new product debut.

Carlie gave the talk and shared the good news. There were loud cheers, as everyone knew they had done their part in making the product a success. Ted looked at Rick to see what his response was. Rick looked at Carlie and then looked down.

Ted decided right then and there that he didn't like Rick at

all. He didn't trust him and felt he was up to no good. He just
didn't know what. Just then, Savannah leaned over to Ted and
whispered "SAM's identity is about to be revealed." Savannah
looked down at the ring she had put on before walking in to the
room. It was the first time she had worn it publicly at work and it
felt good. She was too distracted to hear Ted's response to what
she had just told him.

When Ted heard her, he immediately leaned in and said, "I
don't think it is a good idea" but the warning had fallen on deaf
ears.

Something bad was brewing and Ted didn't know who the
players were. He knew he hadn't mentioned anything to Savannah and wished now that he would have. He stood up feigning an
important phone call and motioned to Savannah to follow him.
He was going to tell her, right now. He just had to. Savannah obediently followed meeting Jim's quizzical stare with one of her own.
She shook her head "no" as she left the room. Jim got the message.
Outside Ted took Savannah and whisked her down the hall.

"What's going on?" she said. "Ted, you are acting very
strange." As Ted started to tell her what he had been piecing
together, Rick suddenly appeared saying that Jim had an
announcement that he wanted everyone to hear. With that he
herded Ted and Savannah back down the hall and into the conference room. Jim's eyes lit up. He walked over to where Savannah
sat down and said, "I want to share this special moment with all of
you. Savannah and I have been dating for some time now. I have
asked her to marry me and she has accepted."

The room burst out in applause and hoots of congratulations.
Immediately, everyone got up and gave Savannah hugs and either
shook Jim's hand or gave him a slap on the back. In the midst of it
all, Savannah tried to find where Carlie was but she was nowhere
to be found. She looked at Jim who was grinning from ear to ear
and enjoying the congratulatory remarks that his staff was giving.
She looked for Ted and as their eyes met, his warning message that

she hadn't heard earlier came screaming to her head now loud and clear. In a panic she wondered why he had said that and whisked her out of the room. Did he know about Carlie and Jim? Somehow she didn't think he did. Savannah wondered what was wrong as she saw Ted walk towards the door. He seemed to be looking for someone.

Ted was indeed looking for someone – Two someone's to be exact: Carlie and Rick who had disappeared right after the news had been announced. Although he didn't know about the family tie that Carlie and Jim had, he thought it odd that two key players to the company did not stop and congratulate the happy couple. In fact, they were the *only* ones that had left the room. He thought they were up to something and he desperately wanted to talk to Savannah. He just didn't seem to be able to get the opportunity.

CHAPTER
TWENTY-EIGHT

The next couple of months were a whirlwind with planning the wedding and gearing up for the summer fruit season, which was very busy, more so at the individual plant locations then at the headquarters in Santa Barbara.

Jim had been flying back and forth to each of the five plant locations to make sure things were running smoothly. Besides the Santa Barbara, Boulder and Lancaster plants that he routinely visited, the plants in Minnesota and Alabama were also busy this time of year. Although they were smaller plants specializing in just the fruits and vegetables that grew heartily in their regions, the summer season was busy for everyone.

Savannah had been talking to Trish and trying to arrange a place to meet. It had been a very hot summer and Trish and Bill were definitely ready to go somewhere to get out of the heat.

Late one afternoon in early August, Savannah and Jim were talking about their upcoming wedding. They had tentatively booked a small venue in a nearby hotel. Nothing fancy, just a nice ceremony in a little cove on the beach followed by a small dinner reception in the hotel banquet room.

On a whim, Savannah suggested that instead of having the wedding in Santa Barbara, they should get married on the lake in Lake Tahoe. Since only a handful of people would be in attendance anyway, it would be a perfect getaway for everyone and then they could all spend a few days enjoying Lake Tahoe and its surrounding areas. Although Bette had been working on wedding plans, it had mostly been decorations that could be moved to any location.

Jim thought about it for a moment and decided it was a great idea. Savannah hadn't really been too excited about the venue they had picked but she came to life with the idea of a Tahoe wedding on the lake. She realized then that it had been the kind of wedding she wanted all along.

They decided that they would get married the weekend after Labor Day and called to see what dates and times were available. As it turned out, their choices were either a Friday late afternoon wedding cruise or a Sunday afternoon wedding cruise. Both options were on a smaller yacht that worked out perfectly since they didn't expect more than 20 people to attend the wedding.

Savannah called Trish to see if they were up for a trip to Lake Tahoe in mid-September. Trish jumped at the idea and when Savannah said the wedding would be on a Friday late in the afternoon she said it sounded perfect. They had decided to rent two townhouses in Tahoe Keys. Jim and Savannah invited Bette and Ted over to tell them the news. They too thought it was a great idea and Bette said that her wedding decorations would be perfect on the yacht.

As the four of them sat at the table, they went over the list of guests. There would be about 20 in all and included Jackie and Ron, Trish and Bill, and six to ten coworkers. Jim mentioned that he had asked Carlie to attend as well and asked her if there was a guest she would like to bring. Carlie had said that she would love to come but would be by herself. When Ted heard that news he was puzzled, but since he hadn't had time to talk to Savannah, he let it go. Bob and his wife were flying in from Lancaster. With the decision that the venue had now been moved to Lake Tahoe, they realized that they had to get the invitations out right away to give people time to plan.

Bette and Savannah created a beautiful invitation that included a weekend stay in Tahoe, courtesy of the bride and groom. Invitations went out by the end of the week and RSVPs were collected quickly. Everyone was able to come and Savannah was very excited.

Although the wedding would be small, it would be elegant and still have some traditional moments, like the first dance, the first bite of cake and the pictures. Everything came together smoothly and rather quickly, and before Savannah knew it, her wedding was just a week away.

"One more week before I am Mrs. James Mullen," she said out loud to her reflection as she looked in the mirror and smiled. She couldn't be any happier.

CHAPTER TWENTY-NINE

Trish and Jackie had really wanted to have a bachelorette party for Savannah and Savannah had given them each other's phone numbers to coordinate the event. They decided to do it on Wednesday night, two days before the wedding. Trish had flown in to Santa Barbara and was staying with Savannah. On Friday, Bill would fly in to Sacramento and then take a small plane to Tahoe.

Jackie was coming over and then they were taking a cab down to the beachfront to have dinner. After dinner they planned to walk over to a new little club that had just opened. As they were getting ready, Trish opened a bottle of wine and turned on some music. They were laughing and talking, and by the time Jackie got there, the bottle of wine was empty. She had brought one with her and opened it right away to catch up.

Finally they were ready to go. Savannah was wearing a beautiful hot pink short dress that was strapless and had a sweetheart neckline. The ladies had bought her a sash that said "Bride-To-Be" on it. Trish and Jackie also wore sundresses and the ladies looked like they were ready for a night on the town. Jackie had called a cab that was now waiting at the curb outside their door.

It was a short cab ride and the beachfront was hopping, especially for a Wednesday evening. The air was warm and the slight breeze coming from the ocean was welcoming. They ate lobster tail at a beachfront restaurant, and then headed down the street to the club. Jackie ran into a few other friends and the six of them sat together and had a great time. Over in the corner was a karaoke machine and everyone was getting up and singing. Savannah, who was normally shy, had enjoyed a Long Island Ice Tea and dragged the girls up on the stage to sing a song. They sang a song about girls wanting to have fun and they had the whole club singing with them by the end of the song. They sang another song about going to a chapel and did quite well harmonizing and everything.

As the evening wound down the girls walked back down the street to the waiting cab. The night was still beautiful and shy Savannah had just experienced a night that she had only read about in magazines.

As she lay down in bed that night, she and Trish talked about the amazing evening. Trish looked over at her friend as she drifted off to sleep. A huge smile plastered her face.

CHAPTER THIRTY

Savannah woke up on her wedding day to the sun shining bright. They had all arrived at their Tahoe destination the day before and she and Trish had been up very late the night before talking about everything that had happened. Savannah was not one for parties but had enjoyed the girls' night out immensely.

Her co-workers had thrown a wedding shower for Jim and her before they left town, and they had received more things then they could ever possibly use. Savannah was so happy. She still couldn't believe that she was getting married. At 30 years old she felt like her life couldn't be any more perfect.

As she and Trish sat on the deck of their room overlooking the lake and drinking coffee, they reminisced about their lives and the important people that had crossed their paths and made them who they were. Just then there was a knock on the door. Savannah opened the door to find Jackie's smiling face with a box full of bagels and cream cheese. She also brought Savannah a beautiful pair of dangly pearl and diamond earrings for her "borrowed" item to wear at the wedding.

Savannah showed Jackie her dress, which was hanging in the other room. It was a beautiful white mermaid type dress that had a sweetheart neckline and buttons all the way down the back. The train wasn't too long, and when cinched up at the back allowed for moving around with ease. She would be wearing a netted veil that laid just slightly over one eye.

They finished their coffee and took showers (Jackie was getting ready there as well), and prepared for the salon staff that was coming in to do their hair and make up. Savannah wore her hair up with loose wisps of hair around her face.

They were transported to the waiting yacht by a white limousine. It was an hour before the wedding and the few expected guests would be arriving soon. Savannah, Trish and Jackie slipped down to the cabin below to complete the final wedding preparations that included getting Savannah into her dress and buttoning the 50 small buttons that trailed down the dress back. Once that task was accomplished, Trish and Jackie finished getting ready and waited with Savannah until it was time. Jim had asked Bill to be his best man. His first choice, Ted, was not available as he was walking Savannah down the isle.

Finally everyone was in place and the harpist was getting ready to play. Ted peaked out to give the cue to start the procession. The harpist started playing a beautiful romantic ballet as Trish walked out. Jackie had been seated next to Ron a little earlier and now they turned to watch as Trish started down the isle.

Savannah asked Ted, "Did Carlie make it here?" Ted turned around and nodded with a puzzled look as to why she had singled Carlie out.

"You do know that Carlie is Jim's aunt don't you? It isn't public knowledge but I thought you knew."

Just then the harpist's song changed to the traditional "Here Comes the Bride" song and Savannah grabbed Ted's arm to start the procession. As the door opened and Ted and Savannah stood there ready to walk, you would have thought that Ted had just seen a ghost. His face was completely white as if he were in shock. And in fact, he was. All the horrific thoughts that had been swirling around in his head now had a motive and a direction. As his eyes scanned the crowd, he met Carlie's icy stare. The flash of a camera broke the jagged stare just in time to get Savannah safely to the bow of the yacht. Jim was waiting there and his eyes were glued to Savannah. In Jim's eyes nothing else mattered.

Savannah and Jim made a beautiful couple and the reception on the yacht was perfect. It was a beautiful late summer/early fall evening and the twinkling of lights on the lake created a beautiful backdrop. Dinner was served inside with unlimited wine. Music was playing first as background music then later for dancing. Although the group was small, they were a lively group and dancing went on until the ship docked at 10:00 p.m.

Two limos were waiting to take the guests back to the townhouses. Jim and Savannah had not only paid for accommodations for everyone but had also picked up the tab for transportation to and from the yacht. Guests had arrived via the same limos and were happy to have safe transportation back.

Jim and Savannah reached their room at 11:00 p.m. They had experienced an amazing day and they were now husband and wife. The honeymoon suite was equipped with every romantic thing you could possibly imagine, but their favorite was the heart shaped Jacuzzi bathtub. Before long they were sitting in the tub drinking champagne and eating chocolate covered strawberries. From there they retired to a queen sized bed with satin sheets and a down comforter. The canopy was made of tulle material and Savannah felt like royalty as she slid in between the sheets. Their lovemaking was passionate, and Savannah wondered how it could keep getting better and better with each experience. Their wedding night ended with Savannah wrapped snuggly in Jim's arms.

Saturday was eventful – relaxing on the beach, walking through an Arts and Wine Festival, and taking a ride up the Gondola. Most everyone had stayed together and ended up having a nice dinner and wrapping up the evening watching an outdoor concert.

Sunday morning, after breakfast, the group said their

goodbyes and parted in separate cars. Most everyone drove the eight-hour trip home but Jim and Savannah and Trish and Bill went to Sacramento where Bill and Trish caught a flight home. Actually, Bill and Trish were headed home and Jim and Savannah were headed to Italy to begin their European honeymoon.

Bill and Trish barely made their flight but Trish and Savannah managed a tearful goodbye anyway. Savannah and Jim were spending the night at the airport hotel and leaving first thing Monday morning.

Monday morning, after their plane was safely in the air, Savannah looked out the window and watched the ground become more and more distant. She thought about her new life so far away from where she had grown up. She lived in a beautiful city with amazing weather, she had a great job that was challenging and fulfilling, she had great friends and was married to the man of her dreams. She leaned over then to rest her head on Jim's shoulder and looked up and asked, "Will you ever answer to 'SAM' again?"

He leaned down and chuckled as he whispered, "God I love you Savannah." She smiled contently and settled in for the long trip ahead.

CHAPTER
THIRTY-ONE

Time passed and life was hectic. Savannah had moved into Jim's condo upon returning from their honeymoon, and she had been busy putting the female decorating touches around the house. She didn't want to do too much as they were looking to buy a house in the near future. They needed more space now that a little one was on the way, a result of honeymoon passion.

Jim and Savannah were both so excited. Savannah had just turned 31 and felt it was time to start a family. Jim was going to be a great dad, nothing like the one she'd had, and for that she was very thankful.

She had a rough first trimester and by month five the doctor had pulled her out of work for the duration of the pregnancy. She wasn't on bed rest, just a reduced daily schedule in order to assure the health of both her baby and herself.

Ted and Bette saw her often, but Ted never discussed the huge problems he was encountering at work. He did not want to do anything to put additional stress on Savannah, and he knew the drama he was encountering at work would send her over the top.

But he also knew he needed to do something. They were

behind in production because Rick had made some modifications to the original line template and now the tooling was all messed up. The processing line for the large commercial piece was not working and two companies had already backed out because of the delays. Ted had met with Carlie and, although she seemed a little concerned, she would not confront Rick to get the problem resolved. Finally, in exasperation, Ted suggested having Bob fly in again to fix the problem and get production back on track. She agreed with his suggestion and Ted thought she looked a little relieved.

Samuel James tumbled into the world early morning May 15th. Labor had been long and intense but once she was fully dilated, he arrived in minutes! At 8 lbs 3 oz he was the most magnificent thing Savannah had ever seen and as the nurse handed the cleanly swaddled bundle of joy to Jim, Savannah snapped a mental picture of the two of them. It was a sight like no other and a tear streamed down her cheek.

Samuel (Sammy) was a good baby and Jim and Savannah were consumed with being the best parents they could possibly be. They had bought a small house in Mission Canyon, a suburb of Santa Barbara, and were happy and content. Savannah went in to the office one day a week while Bette watched Sammy. Ron and Jackie were Jim and Savannah's closest friends with small kids so the four of them, along with the kids, spent a lot of time together. Ron never wanted to talk about work as he felt that his free time was to be spent with family and friends, not dwelling on the problems at work.

But, the problems were becoming more apparent with every passing month. Ron knew about the two cancelled orders due to the production problems but he didn't understand the expenses that were being made. He mentioned it to Carlie once, but she had dismissed it with the comment "you have to spend money in order to make money."

He wished Jim were more hands on like he used to be in the

beginning. He and Jackie had worked in the Boulder Colorado plant but had been given an opportunity to work at the "new" Santa Barbara plant. They had jumped at the chance to move to California and begin a new life adventure. That was when the company was small and Jim was in charge. Ron had moved up in the company and upon finishing his degree, obtained the position of controller for the company. The timing had been perfect because shortly after that Ryder had been born and Jackie was able to stay home. That was almost four years ago and Ron had seen the company grow by leaps and bounds. Only now it seemed like it was really faltering and he didn't know who to talk to since Carlie, his boss and the one supposedly in charge, seemed not to care. He wondered if he should talk to Jim. Then he had a brilliant idea. He would talk to Ted about it. Ted was a good man with a smart head on his shoulders. He was managing the Production Department and must have knowledge of what was going on. Ron would confide in him and see if Ted could share some insight and enlighten him. He needed some concrete numbers to show Ted and had decided to wait a while longer to gather evidence. *I hope I am wrong,* he thought. But in his gut he knew he wasn't.

CHAPTER THIRTY-TWO

Savannah cherished every moment she spent with Sammy and loved the way her little boy reacted to things. For example, every night when she was reading him a story and rocking him to sleep they would hear a train whistle in the far distance. Even if his eyes were closed he would open them and look at Savannah. As he got older and started to say a few words he would whisper, "what's that?" And Savannah would laugh and tell him "a choo choo train Sammy." He would smile and snuggle up in Savannah's arms and fall asleep.

Savannah loved being a mom and she and Sammy did everything together. Since Jim was still traveling often, Savannah would make up different games to keep little Sammy busy. Since Sammy loved trains so much they bought him a toy train set for Christmas that even whistled. Sammy was fascinated with the train and as Sammy grew they spent hours changing the track pattern to make the train go in different directions.

The days turned in to months and before they knew it, Sammy was turning three. Jim came home from work one day and told Savannah about a surprise he had for Sammy's birthday. He had heard of a special park where you could ride a real train. They picked a bright sunny Saturday for the outing.

Sammy was so excited when he found out he was going for a ride on a real choo choo train that he could barely sleep. When they arrived early Saturday morning at the park, the conductor was just starting his day and, since no one else was around, gave Sammy and his parents a tour of all the various cars and what they were used for. They even had a meal car. The conductor gave Sammy a little conductor's hat at the end of the tour and let him blow the whistle. Sammy was so excited he couldn't stop talking about it as they made their way to their assigned seats. As the train started moving, Sammy's eyes grew wide and as he looked out the window and saw the people waving goodbye, he stood and waved his biggest wave and was grinning from ear to ear.

They rode up the coast and the train's whistle would blow now and then. Every time he heard the whistle, Sammy's eyes would light up. The train ride lasted a little over two hours. Toward the end of the trip, Sammy was falling asleep just as the train entered a mountain tunnel. The change in the engine sound broke the lull of the white noise that had been singing Sammy to sleep and he looked at Savannah in a panic. Before she could respond they were back in daylight and his face took on a relaxed look as he smiled and went back to sleep. Jim laughed at how he could drift off to sleep and commented on how he wished he could do the same.

Truth be told it was getting harder and harder to sleep these days as he felt that something wasn't right at work but he wasn't sure what it was. He was angry with himself for losing that "hands on" approach that he had so long ago. He had stepped away and let Carlie run the show then stepped away even further when Sammy was born. But now, as he traveled among the plants, he got the sense that things were falling apart. He wanted to talk to Savannah about it but didn't want to worry her. He made a mental note that starting Monday he would go back to the basics and find out what was going on. And he would start with Carlie. She had been very distant and distracted and he didn't like it. Maybe that was what was sending him these alarming signals. He would figure it out on Monday.

They got off the train and went to have corn dogs and ice cream at a nearby stand. Sammy proudly sported his conductor's hat and every time he heard the train in the distance, he would look at his mom and dad and smile saying "That's our choo choo train!" It was a great day and as Savannah was reading him his bedtime story that evening, they heard the familiar daily train's whistle in the distance.

Sammy looked up and smiled at his mom and said "What's that?" It was a special phrase that Sammy always said when he heard a train's whistle.

"Our choo choo train Sammy!"

Savannah smiled and hugged him tight and left him to his dreams. He still had a smile on his face when she went in to check on her sleeping bundle. *Everything is perfect,* she thought.

CHAPTER THIRTY-THREE

Monday was the day Savannah went in to the office. She was busy getting ready and packing Sammy's bag for a day at Bette's. She and Jim were talking about the day's events over breakfast when the phone rang. It was a manager from the Boulder Plant and she was in a panic. They had a large client coming in to the office late in the afternoon and their main conveyer belt had stopped working. The mechanics had been trying all weekend but couldn't get it up and running and the client was scheduled to take a tour. That line was the one Jim had installed years ago and he knew it like the back of his hand. He told her he would take the earliest flight he could get and be there soon.

He hung up the phone and packed an overnight bag. Savannah was disappointed but was used to the quick overnight trips to Boulder. That plant was the oldest and had the oldest equipment. Once, when Savannah had gone there with Jim, she suggested that he replace all the equipment. He took offense to that and said that he and his Dad had built the plant and he wanted it to remain intact. She had apologized, as she hadn't realized how important the plant was to him. She understood the sentimental aspect of it.

As he was packing now, she smiled at him, at the concern on his face and at the heroic way he was planning on going in to save the day.

They kissed at the door and he explained he would sit at the airport on stand by until he got a flight – the same thing he always did for these quick flights. He said he would text her with the times and flight numbers as soon as he knew them. With that, they parted and went off in different directions.

As Savannah piled all of Sammy's things into the back of the car, she was happy that they had made a wise car purchase long before Sammy had arrived. She had opted for a small SUV anticipating someday having kids and wanting to make sure that there was ample space to store everything needed for kids. Four doors were a must even though it had taken away the sporty feel she had originally wanted. She was always the practical one and today she was glad she had been as she helped Sammy into his car seat and buckled him in safely.

Bette loved to watch Sammy. She looked forward to seeing him every week and today was no exception. Usually, Savannah didn't see Ted as he would already be at work, but today he was there waiting for Savannah and, if she was reading him correctly, something was wrong. Whatever it was, Bette apparently hadn't caught on. She was smiling as she bent down to greet Sammy and receive "Grandma" hugs and kisses. Savannah gave Sammy a hug and kiss goodbye, thanked Bette with a hug and left with Ted to go to the office. He said he would drive as he was planning on leaving early today and could drop Savannah off at the house. She declined to carpool as she had some errands to run at lunch but agreed to follow him to a nearby coffee shop to talk.

As they sat down and ordered coffee, Savannah could tell that something was bothering him. Ted seemed like he was ready to burst. He pulled out some papers from his brief case and laid them on the table. They were budget spreadsheets that Ron had given him when they had met the night before. There were concrete facts about over spending and low sales as well as some unaccounted for losses. Savannah stared at the spreadsheets then back at Ted.

OMG, she thought. *Is this a joke?* One look at Ted's face and she realized, this was *not* a joke. It was more like a horrific nightmare. Ted then went on to tell her all the other facts about Carlie and Rick, their "relationship" whatever it was, Rick's lack of engineering experience and the observations that Bob had witnessed at the Lancaster Plant. He also said that when Savannah had thrown him that bomb about Carlie being Jim's aunt, it had sent him in to a tailspin and redirected his thoughts. Today, however, he felt he had enough facts, because he heard that Carlie and Rick were planning an extended vacation very soon and he figured they were taking the company profits with them.

Savannah was in shock. She thought back over the last three years and how she and Carlie had become more and more distant. Actually it was since the engagement over four years ago. She had avoided Savannah at all costs and thankfully Savannah had been able to do her job anyway. Ted had been the go-between and although Savannah thought it odd that Carlie wanted nothing to do with Sammy, after talking it over with Jim, he had said that was just the way she was. Savannah was sad with that but she had dismissed the odd "auntie" behavior.

Savannah had no idea about Carlie's relationship with Rick. She really didn't know Rick too well since, come to think of it, he had also kept his distance. She knew everyone else at the Santa Barbara location except maybe a handful of workers, Rick being one of them.

Ted then said, "I don't like him Savannah. He doesn't know what he is doing and I think he is bad news. If Carlie is already on the edge, he would be the one to push her to do something sinister since she is head over heels for him."

Savannah remembered that Jim had told her how Carlie had lost her husband very tragically. She had been deeply in love with him, and her whole life had changed after his death. She had moved back home and embarked on a new career. Jim had mentioned that she never really dated and just sort of existed. Savannah felt sorry for her and had tried several times to get to know her, only to be pushed away. With this new information she could see that Carlie was probably so lonely that she could be swept off her feet fairly easily and talked in to a bad situation for companionship. Rick was a nice looking man for his age and she knew he could be a smooth talker. He had probably wrapped Carlie around his finger to get what he wanted. Ted said from what he could tell, this had been years in the making and although it had appeared to Ted that Carlie was a little uneasy at times, she had turned a blind eye when Ted was pointing out the obvious. He had noticed a change in her; subtle at first, but now becoming more and more, what was the word he was looking for – desperate – that was it.

After meeting with Ron the evening before and getting the cold hard facts, he felt he was ready to unveil what he thought was going on. He had also conducted some research on Rick and couldn't find where he had even graduated from college. It wasn't the fact that he didn't have a college education that concerned Ted. It was more the fact that he wasn't an engineer and had somehow been hired as one.

Further research revealed that Carlie had been the sole person to hire him and he probably had started schmoozing her from that moment on. Ted had planned to talk to Jim when they dropped off Sammy and had been rather surprised when only Savannah appeared at the door. They always carpooled together on Mondays. But today, since Jim was now on his way to Colorado, Ted thought he had better tell Savannah because she would have Jim's ear sooner then anyone else, and Ted was fearful that the demise of the company could happen any day. It was a delicate situation since Carlie was Jim's aunt and he felt that the news would be hard to take. Ted knew that Carlie was involved in whatever he felt was about to happen, but he didn't know to what extent. He also knew that Savannah was a smart lady and would be able to get the message across to Jim gently.

With the spreadsheets laid out in front of her, the script seemed to be writing itself. Savannah realized that she was the lead in the next scene as she was the one that needed to talk to Jim right away. He needed to have this information to get Rick out of there before he lured Carlie in to doing something really bad – like bankrupt the company and take off.

Then she remembered that Jim was at the airport waiting for a flight. She had to move quickly. She grabbed the spreadsheets and told Ted that she was going to the airport to tell Jim about what they suspected was happening and to show him the financial documents. She would make sure Jim got to the office ASAP. The customer that was scheduled to tour the Boulder plant would just have to be rescheduled. The matter at hand was way more important.

Ted told her that he would tell staff she was at an off-site meeting and wished her luck. She was thankful that the airport was just minutes away and Jim hadn't text her yet so he was still sitting at the airport. She rushed to her car and pulled out into commuter traffic. It wasn't too bad but she knew she would have to hurry if she wanted to talk to Jim before he got on a flight.

She got to the last light just as it was turning yellow/red and had to slam on her brakes. It was a big intersection and to go through it would have been running a solid red. She waited patiently for the light to turn green as she was trying to process the information she had just been told. She would have to be very careful with how she presented the information to Jim, as it was his aunt that was either the problem or in trouble. When the light finally changed, she stepped on the gas trying to make up for lost time. The guy crossing the intersection from the other side must not have known how big the intersection was. Unlike Savannah, he chose not to stop at the yellow/red light and slammed right into the driver's side of Savannah's car. She didn't even see it coming. The light turned green and Savannah's world went black.

CHAPTER
THIRTY-FOUR

Jim had finally gotten a flight scheduled to board in 30 minutes. He texted Savannah the information, then called her to say goodbye. Her phone went right to voice mail as if it had been shut off. *That's odd*, he thought. *She never shuts her phone off.* He called again and received the same response.

Trying not to read anything else in to it, he decided to phone Bette to see if Savannah was still there with her and Sammy. Bette said that both Ted and Savannah had left over an hour ago and she thought she had heard them say they were going for coffee.

Jim thanked her and decided to call Ted. He was getting a little worried and decided that he was probably just anxious about what he had waiting for him in Boulder. Ted picked up on the first ring and said "Hi Jim. Savannah told you everything-huh?"

"I haven't talked to Savannah" Jim said and his voice now had an alarming sound in it. "I thought she was with you." Ted changed gears immediately.

"Uh no" he said. "She was going to the airport to see you." Just then another call was coming in to Jim's phone and the last part of Ted's message was broken up.

"I have another call coming in Ted. I will call you right back." Jim sounded distracted as he ended the call.

Ted heard the dial tone in his ear and it took him a minute to separate the sound from the matter at hand. He hung up the phone and dialed Savannah. Voice mail. He left the office and ran to his car. *Please let her be ok,* he prayed. He merged onto the main road only to be stuck in a huge traffic jam. *This is a crazy amount of traffic for this time of day,* he thought. He made a right turn to try to get around the traffic jam and came up on the side street where ambulances and fire engines were screeching their horns to try and make it to an accident scene. Ted pulled over, hopped out of the car and started running. *It couldn't be,* he thought. He turned the corner and his worst fears were confirmed. Savannah's small SUV was lying in two pieces, split apart behind the driver's seat, and an old Ford Truck was close by with the front end folded like an accordion. A large group of people circled around something or someone and Ted ran to the crowd and pushed through. There was a man giving CPR to the victim who lay motionless. Other then a badly broken leg, she looked like she was sleeping and as he knelt down beside her he burst in to tears. Firefighters arrived then with medical equipment and a gurney. Savannah lay motionless but she was breathing. The man had saved her life.

Ted was in the ambulance and calling Jim. Jim's phone went to voice mail. *He must still be on the phone,* Ted thought. He texted Jim and told him not to get on the plane and to call him immediately. Within seconds his phone was ringing and a panicked Jim was on the other end. Ted told him briefly what had happened and told him which hospital they were taking her to. Jim told him he would meet them there shortly. Jim was crying when he hung up.

Through tears of his own, Ted called Bette and told her the news. He said that he would call her later with an update and that Sammy would be spending the next few nights with them.

He hung up the phone and looked at Savannah. The EMT driver said that she was unconscious and had suffered head trauma and a broken leg. They were not able to set the leg as it was badly broken and would have to be operated on and set at the hospital. The extent of the head trauma would be revealed through an MRI, but the hospital had been notified that they were coming and they would be ready. Savannah's body was in shock. Ted was in shock too. Moments after they wheeled Savannah into the MRI room Jim burst through the door.

"Where is she?" Jim questioned. "What happened?"

Ted hadn't analyzed the whole thing but had given the police officers his card and told them to call him later. He said it looked like the truck had broadsided Savannah and she had flown out of the car. He had momentarily forgotten that Savannah's car had been split in two by the impact of the heavy truck. The fact that Savannah had survived at the scene was a miracle in itself.

~~~~~

Hours went by as Ted and Jim waited for results of Savannah's MRI. All Ted could tell Jim was what the EMT had *thought* was the diagnosis. He wasn't a doctor and they hadn't run any tests. But he could see her broken leg, and the fact that there was no outward bleeding and she was still breathing meant some kind of internal trauma.

Both Jim and Ted's phones were ringing constantly as word got out about the accident. Ted asked Bette to call Jackie, Trish and Bob but other than that, he didn't take any calls from anyone. Jim put his phone on silent and quietly prayed for a positive outcome.

Several hours later, the doctor came out to talk to the two men. Both had been waiting for hours now and were worried, tired, and hungry. Other than a cup of coffee, neither of them had eaten anything since the accident.

Savannah's diagnosis was sketchy. She definitely had a broken leg, which had been operated on and then set. It would heal nicely. She had suffered a major head injury as she had been ejected from the car when it split in two. The only thing that had saved her was her bulky purse, which had flown out with her and provided a minimal, but life-saving cushion as her head hit the asphalt.

There was no internal bleeding, but the extent of the head injury had yet to be determined. She was put in intensive care in a medically induced coma to be watched for the night. Staff said they would allow Savannah to have visitors in about an hour, once they processed her paperwork and got her settled in her room. Jim and Ted took that opportunity to run to the cafeteria to get a bite to eat. It was well after dinnertime and the food had been picked over. They each grabbed a pre-made turkey sandwich, some chips and a soda and sat silently eating in the cold cafeteria. Each was lost in thought about how sad he felt. After the food was gone, Ted looked at Jim and saw a heartbroken man. Savannah completed him and now she laid motionless upstairs with her life hanging precariously by a thread. Ted said that after they saw Savannah he would go home and get a change of clothes for Jim and bring it back. He also told him not to worry about Sammy, that he would be well taken care of. He said Savannah was most important and he should stay with her. Jim smiled a grateful smile and stood up. Ted followed as they made their way silently to the intensive care unit.

CHAPTER THIRTY-FIVE

It was eerily quiet as they walked pass the beds in the Intensive Care ward. Other than the beeping of the heart monitors and the up and down of some breathing apparatuses, the halls were deathly silent. Jim thought he was going to pass out and grabbed on to a curtain to steady himself. He couldn't believe what had happened and he was having a hard time coping. Ted, who was twice his age, was there for him and was holding up like a rock. Just then a nurse appeared from behind a curtain.

"Mr. Mullen? Jim Mullen?"

"Yes," Jim answered.

"Your wife is right here." She then turned to Ted. "Are you her father?"

"Uh, yes." Ted said. There was no way he was going to be kicked out.

"Ok." The nurse acknowledged. "Savannah is in a medically induced coma to allow her body to heal a little bit. She is quite banged up but she is hanging in there. Don't be alarmed when you see her." With that, she pushed the curtain back.

They both stood staring at Savannah too traumatized by what

they saw to move. They recovered at the same time and each went to a side of her bed. Her head had been partially shaved and was severely swollen at the bare spot. Her face was black and blue and hardly recognizable. Her eyes were swollen and her lids were closed. Other than the cast on her leg, the rest of her body was unharmed. Not even a scratch.

Jim reached for Savannah's hand then leaned over and gently kissed her lips. An unmanaged tear escaped his eye and rolled down her cheek. Ted held her other hand. After what seemed like seconds, the nurse came in and told them they had to step out for a few minutes, as they had to perform routine checks on her vitals and make sure everything was documented.

Ted took this time to leave and go get Jim a change of clothes. He had phoned Bette on the way to Jim's and had gotten a list of things to pick up for Sammy as well. It was late and he was beat. He knew after going back by the hospital to drop Jim's things off, he would have to go home and get some sleep or he would be no good to anyone.

He thought about the horrible day's events and recalled the grizzly car crash scene. He hadn't even seen the other driver and had no idea if he had even made it. He still didn't know what happened either. Given the number of witnesses that had been surrounding Savannah, Ted was sure he would find out the whole truth soon enough. A tear escaped his eye at the thought of her lying in the street. For a split second he had thought she was dead and the relief that flooded him when he saw a shallow breath was overwhelming. He quickly gathered the needed clothing for both Jim and Sammy and was again back in his car. After dropping the items off at the hospital for Jim, he thought for a minute about work. He realized, with a jolt, that Jim still hadn't been told what was going on and the eminent fall of his company. He had to do something to protect everyone from the harm that he suspected Rick and Carlie were getting ready to do.

Bette greeted him at the door and they embraced each other a long while. He then went in to check on the sweet little boy who could possibly be without a mother soon. Sammy slept peacefully not knowing that his life was about to change drastically. It was too much and as Ted quietly closed the door he broke down in the hallway and wept uncontrollably. He was on his knees in a ball when Bette found him – she had come to investigate the unfamiliar sound she had heard in the hall. She rubbed his back and tried to console him but he just couldn't compose himself. Bette had never seen Ted like this and she was concerned. She wondered if he was having a nervous breakdown. Even when his parents had passed he had handled it better than this. What she didn't know was that not only was Ted worried about Savannah; he was worried that the company he worked for was about to be sabotaged. He felt like the world was on his shoulders and he could no longer carry it. He was at his limit. Ted was a broken man.

CHAPTER
THIRTY-SIX

Tuesday mid morning Ron was pacing his office floor. He had heard about Savannah and knew that Jim was definitely preoccupied. He had tried to reach Ted and had left several messages but had not received a call back. His secretary had told him that a meeting had been scheduled to go over job duties while Jim and Savannah were not available. He also got wind that Carlie was going out of town and realized that the bomb was about to drop. He made a decision and did what he had to do. He had high-level financial authority and used it now to the fullest extent. He called the bank and had all company funds frozen until further notice.

He used the excuse of the medical emergency of the owner's wife and that seemed to suffice with the bank. He had checked all balances before making the requests and had printed out current balance information on every account the company had. He knew that he and Jim were the only ones that could release the hold and he verified that the authorization policy they had put in place so long ago was still in place with the bank. Thank God it was.

With everything safely done Ron breathed a sigh of relief just as the phone started ringing. A hoarse but recognizable voice was on the other end. Ted had finally succumbed to exhaustion and, after sobbing for hours, had fallen asleep. When he had opened his eyes the sky was bright and he grabbed his phone to see about any updates. He saw all the missed calls from Ron. A brief text from Jim stating "no change" had told the story at the hospital.

Ron sounded confident as he relayed the move he had made to Ted. As he heard himself say the words out loud he became stronger still, knowing that he had done the right thing. Ted applauded his quick thinking and agreed that funds being frozen for a few days wouldn't hurt the company at all. Ted said that he would attend the 3:00 p.m. meeting and provide his *own* update of what was going on with the company if need be. Ted felt confident that if Carlie and Rick tried to pull a fast one and Ted made an issue of it, he felt that Carlie would back down. He didn't know that for sure, but he had a hunch and right now that was good enough.

He got off the phone with Ron and had a new sense of purpose. Having a smart man at his side, he knew they could weather any storm, or hurricane, that seemed to be on the horizon. He showered quickly and before long was dressed and went out to the kitchen to see Bette and Sammy.

Apparently, they had spent the morning at the park to allow Ted to sleep peacefully. As Ted walked through the kitchen entryway, Bette was surprised to see him up and dressed but relieved that he looked like his old self. Ted looked at Sammy and realized how much he resembled Savannah although he had his father's green eyes. He had his mother's brown hair and olive skin and he truly was an adorable little boy.

After lunch, and with renewed energy, Ted headed to the hospital to check on Savannah and Jim. She was still in a medically induced coma and sleeping peacefully, but Jim was a train wreck. Ted convinced him to go home for a little while to get something to eat and he would pick him up and bring him back in the evening. Jim reluctantly agreed but then he realized that he hadn't seen his little boy and desperately wanted to go see him. He also realized that he couldn't let Sammy see him in his current state.

Jim drove home with his mind in a fog and coming home to an empty house was devastating. As the door closed behind him he collapsed and let all the sadness and fear that he'd kept bottled up inside over the last 24 hours have the stage. He was exhausted and depleted. He fell asleep sobbing right on the living room carpet.

CHAPTER
THIRTY-SEVEN

A week and a half had gone by and they still had Savannah medically sedated. She would be in that state until the doctors felt it was safe enough for her to be awake and moving. Until then they needed to make sure she stayed very still to help her head heal. She had suffered a major head injury and although a complete diagnosis would not be known for some time, they knew that her body still needed to lay completely still. They would not know the extent of the damage until she was allowed to come out of the coma. In the meantime her bruises were healing nicely. The swelling had gone down and the black and blue marks were beginning to fade. Jim spent most every day and night there but took time to be with Sammy every day. When Sammy asked where his mommy was, Jim had all he could do not to break down. Instead he said she would not be home for a little while but would hopefully be back soon.

Meanwhile a decision had to be made about when and what they were going to tell Sammy. Jim, Ted, and Bette were trying to decide how to tell him. They planned to wait to see what the final diagnosis was and then they would call the pediatrician and get his opinion as well.

They had received the police report on the accident at the beginning of the week and were shocked that Savannah was even alive. The other driver hadn't been as lucky. But, if Savannah came off the sedation and was brain dead, who would really be the lucky one?

According to the driver that had been directly behind Savannah, she had stopped abruptly to not run a yellow/red light however, when the light turned green, she took off immediately. The driver in the Ford truck had picked up speed in order to try to get through the light and had entered the intersection on a solid red slamming right into the driver's side of Savannah's car. Although Savannah had been wearing a seat belt, it had unlatched when the car split in two and she had been ejected from the car on impact. She was saved from immediate death by a large bag that had flown out of the car with her and cushioned her fall, ever so slightly, but perhaps enough to save her life.

The other driver had not been wearing a seatbelt and the sheer force of the impact had crushed him against the steering wheel, killing him instantly. The policeman at the scene and the emergency room doctor at the hospital had each said that it was doubtful that either one of the victims knew what hit them.

Another week went by and Jim was trying to put on a strong face for Sammy and keep a somewhat normal routine. Sammy spent a lot of time at Ted and Bette's house, which he loved.

As one week turned into the next Sammy was asking for mommy less and less. This concerned Jim because he didn't want him ever to forget his mother. He would show him pictures and Sammy always smiled but no longer asked where she was. He was in pre-school and that helped, giving him something to focus on and talk about. It broke Jim's heart but he was happy that he no longer had to stretch the truth about his wife.

Jim still went to see Savannah every day hoping that each day would be the day the doctors would say she had improved enough to come completely out of her deep sleep. They had decided to take her out gradually to see if her body responded positively.

Jim had met with both Ted and Ron and had all the pieces of the puzzle regarding the embezzlement issue. Because of everything that had happened, and the fact they couldn't get to the company money, the getaway scheme Rick and Carlie had been planning had been foiled and Jim had been able to handle the problem.

He had been in shock not wanting to admit that Carlie would ever do anything detrimental to him or the company that she loved so much. He had called her in his office and they had gone round and round about what was going on. She tried making excuses and seemed to be fumbling with her words. When asked about Rick's lack of ability to do his job she seemed surprised. Then she claimed that the equipment was not set up properly so Rick had had to try to piecemeal it (unsuccessfully) together to try to get it to work. Because Jim was well versed in the production end of equipment, he wasn't buying what she said and called her on it.

She broke down then and told him everything – that shortly after Rick was hired they had started dating. Rick had been hired just before talks began to purchase the new "Cutting Edge" product. Rick had been following the success of *The Ripe and Ready Fruit Company* and knew the company was solid. After being hired and learning of the "Cutting Edge" patent that the company had just purchased, he felt he had hit the jackpot and decided that he wanted to get a share of the profits that the company was sure to see. He then pursued Carlie heavily and she had been flattered and smitten by him. As time went by he worked his way into knowing all the details of how the company was run. He had charmed her for a couple of years and she hadn't even realized that he had been manipulating her while he learned all about what made the company tick. He had asked her leading questions on more than one occasion and, because she seemed to be blinded by her attraction to him, gave out more information then she ever should have. He learned that *The Ripe and Ready Fruit Company* was worth millions. The company itself had just recently gone public and their stock was now sold on the New York Stock Exchange.

When Carlie realized how much she had divulged over the years without even knowing it, she tried to back up and retract things. The more she did this however, the more Rick pushed. Beginning to panic, she had tried to break it off with him. He quickly figured out that she had caught on to what he was trying to do. He began to pressure her into staying in the relationship saying that he would press sexual harassment charges against her if she broke it off with him. She had panicked then and kept quiet.

As the time for the "getaway" had approached she had become more and more distant from everyone including Jim. She hadn't been able to look him in the eye as she was so humiliated and scared. Unfortunately, the accident had been a godsend for the company as it had forced both Ron's and Ted's hands and ultimately saved the company and helped Carlie as well.

She was teary eyed as she told Jim how sorry she was. She told him that she was scared and didn't know what Rick would do. Jim called the company attorney right away. No one was going to blackmail him or his aunt. He would make sure of that.

CHAPTER
THIRTY-EIGHT

It was dark, and she was running. At least she thought she was running. She seemed to be in a tunnel but she could see the light at the end. And then it was dark again.

It was the middle of July and it had already been a long summer. Rick had been fired and of course tried to sue the company. He had a really good lawyer but Jim's lawyers were better and they won the legal battle.

A new engineer had been hired and the company was in full swing for the summer season. Sammy was doing nicely and had adapted well to his new routine. Savannah had been lifted out of the medically induced coma and had woken up to see Jim staring down lovingly at her. His smile was magnetic, however she didn't recognize him, and other then smiling back with a friendly smile she didn't respond to him at all.

Savannah was suffering from neurological amnesia and couldn't remember much of anything at first. As Jim came to see her every day she was slowly starting to remember bits and pieces of him and their relationship. She had been moved to a medical facility where she could recuperate under a doctor's watchful eye.

The doctor had preferred a supervised recovery due to the severity of the head injury. Jim had been told that it would be a long process and to be patient. Her leg had healed and she walked every day to regain the muscle she had lost. She had no recollection of the last few years of her life but, since she recognized Ted and had not taken too long to remember Jim, the doctors were hopeful that, in time, her memory would come back completely.

One afternoon in late August, Savannah and Jim were walking in the courtyard of the facility that she still resided in. Jim decided to talk about Sammy. She hadn't asked about him at all and Jim realized that she probably didn't know he existed. He wanted his family back together and he wanted Sammy to have his mother back.

Just as he was about to bring it up they heard a loud screeching of tires as a car stopped just short of hitting another car. Savannah jumped extremely high and then took off running. It caught Jim off guard and when he finally reached her they were both panting and out of breath. Savannah was visually frightened and it took a long time for her to settle down. The nurse actually gave her something to help her unwind and Jim stayed with her until she fell asleep.

Savannah was dreaming – again. She had been having the same dream for a month or so now but couldn't figure out what the dream meant. She was running through a tunnel. Running away from someone or something. Often times she would wake up right before she reached the end of the tunnel. When she had those dreams she would wake up confused and scared. Other times, she would have the same dream but she would make it all the way to the end of the tunnel and then she would see him. Their eyes would meet and they would melt her heart. Then she would wake up. After those dreams she was happy and content. Jim began to recognize which dream she'd had by her behavior. She was getting stronger every day and would be going home in the next week or two. He was worried that she wouldn't be able to handle the fact that she was a mother. After all, it had been three months since the accident and she hadn't asked about Sammy or even mentioned him once. It was clear that she didn't know about him.

After talking with the doctor it was decided that the best way to help Savannah gain her memory would be to take her home and reacquaint her with things. Trish had invited her to come to Lancaster and the doctor thought it would be a great starting point to help her to remember. The doctor explained that her memory could come back all at once or in pieces, but by the progress she had already made, he predicted that she would make a complete recovery. It would just take time.

CHAPTER THIRTY-NINE

Jim and Savannah boarded the plane for Lancaster at the end of September. Savannah had been home for almost a month, and things were falling into place for her each day. They had decided to take the doctor's advice and see if the Lancaster trip would help Savannah remember. She was going to stay with Trish for two weeks and then Jim would fly back out to pick her up.

Savannah had seen pictures of Trish and had recognized her. Jim was hoping that seeing Trish in Savannah's hometown would put another piece of her memory back in to place.

He recalled a few weeks back they were snuggled on the couch and she had leaned over and said, "You smell amazing." He laughed and told her she always use to say that to him. She had blushed and looked away. Sometimes it felt like they had just met. It was exciting in one way but hard in another. They had to take their relationship very slow, as he didn't want to do anything to set her off. The doctor said she was making good progress and if enough different pieces of her memory came back, the missing events would fill back in quickly. That was a big reason he wanted to have Savannah see her hometown roots.

Savannah was still having the dream. It didn't scare her anymore, it made her happy and she felt that the recurring dream was her subconscious trying to help her remember. Although she had other dreams, the one of her in the tunnel was the one she had at least once every three days. She had told Jim about the dream but he couldn't figure out why she was having it over and over again or what it meant. The doctor thought that the dream might be the key to unlocking the missing memory blocks. As time went on, the doctor reiterated that bringing her around familiar things would help. Familiar sights, sounds, faces and places were all important, as any one of them could be the key to unlock her hidden memories.

She had seen Sammy but didn't recognize him. Sammy started to cry because he didn't understand, and that broke Savannah's heart. Jim blamed himself for that. He had thought that Savannah would recognize Sammy right away and had told Sammy that mommy was home and to run up and give her a hug. He had told Savannah that he had a surprise and was just about to tell her that she was going to see her son when Sammy ran into the room saying "Mommy, Mommy" with his arms open wide. When he hugged her she looked at Jim and hugged the strange boy awkwardly. She smiled at him but there was no recognition in her eyes. Sammy had started to cry then and Bette had taken him away.

Savannah had been heartbroken and asked, "Where is his mother?"

When Jim told her that *she* was his mother, she broke down and cried as she felt she had broken his heart unknowingly. She sobbed too because she couldn't remember her precious baby. They had thought it better to wait a little while before having them meet again to allow the hurt that Sammy felt to subside. Meanwhile, he spent a lot of time at Ted and Bette's house. Jim explained to his son that his mom had been hurt and didn't remember lots of things but she was getting better. He was so young he couldn't really understand. Jim said it more to pacify himself. Jim kept reminding Sammy of all the fun things that he and his mom used to do, and told him that they needed to help her get better. Sammy said he was a big boy and he could do that.

Jim was now on a mission to find the key to unlock her memory. He had done extensive research, but because everyone was different and every head injury was different, he was on his own. Actually *they* were on their own as Savannah wanted it just as much as he did.

They had finally reconnected intimately the night before they left for Lancaster and it was just as amazing as it had always been. They had a chemistry that was extremely powerful and Jim was happy that it was still every bit as strong. Savannah had also expressed how electrifying their attraction was and it had opened the gate of her relationship with Joel. Although it was not a good memory, it had opened up a path and unlocked yet another series of memories. Savannah was indeed making progress.

It was good to see Trish and as they ran into each other's arms, the memories of Trish and of their youth flooded Savanna's brain. It was like the sun had come out and she could finally see. And more big news, Trish was pregnant! Very pregnant, due any day, and all of a sudden Savannah was remembering.

Jim was very happy and knew that this trip might be the trigger to get their lives back. As he got on the plane to head to Colorado, he promised God that he would *never* take anything for granted again.

Up in the air Jim was finally able to relax. He thought about what was waiting for him to deal with in Boulder. The plant was doing great. Everything had been righted after the mess Carlie and Rick had caused and business as a whole was booming.

Carlie had moved back to Colorado to head up the Boulder Plant. It was perfect timing because Bryce, the head hauncho at the Boulder Plant, had retired and left a vacant position. Carlie really needed to get away from the drama surrounding her affair with Rick – a shady character hired by a vulnerable middle-aged woman longing for something more. Rick had been the villain and Carlie, while lonely and desperate, was crushed in the process. If she had been at any other company and this happened, she would have been fired on the spot. But Jim couldn't fire her; he didn't have the heart and he knew she was a good person. Unfortunately, she had been so lonely she made bad choices for companionship. She was now seeing a counselor once a week to help her sort out her issues.

Work was good for her. Jim knew that, and already she had made a couple of positive changes. Jim trusted her despite what had occurred earlier and was looking forward to not having to fly to Boulder quite so often. He really wanted to stay in California and focus on his family.

His relationship with Carlie had improved immensely and they finally talked about things other than work. Carlie had met Sammy a few times and loved him dearly. It was like Sammy had brought out a side of her that had been deeply buried. Jim was glad that Sammy had been able to bridge the gap between them and make their family a little bigger. He felt bad that Carlie had never found someone else after the loss of her husband. She was still young enough and there was still time. She just needed to work on herself, which she was doing. He was happy for her.

With all the problems that had occurred with the company and the fact that Jim wanted to be there to help Savannah get better and be the best father he could be to Sammy, Jim had made the decision to close the Alabama and the Minnesota Plants. They were the two smallest plants and had minimal profits at best. At one point he had thought he would expand but he was no longer interested in doing so. Other things were more important.

CHAPTER FORTY

Ted was busy at work. Jim had named him Plant Manager for the Santa Barbara facility and as he thought about it now, he had to laugh. He was actually doing exactly what he didn't want to do – be in charge of a huge plant – but he loved it.

He had a good team working for him. The new engineer that Bob had helped him hire, was energetic and really knew his stuff. He had a wealth of experience and had been highly recommended. In the month he had been there, he had learned everything he needed to do to keep the operation running smoothly. It was Ted's thought that they should expand some of the projects they had in the works, and he was ready and anxious to get going. He even had a few ideas of his own and Ted liked that he had such a go-getter attitude. It was contagious and made everyone work a little harder and be proud of what they did.

Ron was excellent at managing the company's Finance Department and had proven to be a smart dependable guy over and over again. He and his team had shaved off unnecessary expenses and had each division watching their spending. For this reason, they were heading toward one of the highest quarterly profits the company had ever experienced.

Big bonuses were promised if they met or exceeded the

projected quarter net earnings. Bonuses would be given at the end of October after all numbers from the previous quarter were reconciled. The bonus incentive motivated people to do their best and be conscious of their spending. They had never been offered that incentive before and production skyrocketed. Ted had talked to Jim and had told him that money motivates people. Jim laughed and agreed. He had never thought about it like that but was on board with the idea. Of course, it had paid off.

Ted smiled as he realized the company was starting to feel like the old company back in Lancaster and he was proud.

CHAPTER
FORTY-ONE

Trish and Savannah talked non-stop all the way home. Savannah listened as Trish described different events and little by little Savannah began to put the puzzle pieces of her life together. They had spent time getting the nursery ready and Trish was very excited to meet her new little addition. She and Bill had opted not to find out if it was a boy or girl before the baby arrived and that made for an additional aura of excitement.

They had shopped and talked and shopped some more. Trish had driven her around Lancaster indicating various points of interest to help jog her memory. She drove by the house Savannah had lived in with her mom and the elementary school they had attended together. She then drove by the apartment Savannah had lived in before she moved and, ironically enough, the apartment was for rent.

As they walked through the rooms of the apartment a dim memory flashed through Savannah's head. It was as if she was looking through binoculars and she could see things and remember them – almost. The memories were hazy, but they were there – or starting to be there anyway.

Trish kept reminding her of places and events as they continued their journey around Lancaster. One day, they met Bob for lunch. He was very busy these days, as he had been promoted to Plant Manager of the Lancaster Plant. The plant was running smoothly and he loved his new job of overseeing the entire plant. When he saw Savannah, his instinct was to give her a big hug but as he approached her, he hesitated in case she didn't recognize him. Trish reintroduced Bob to Savannah and explained how they knew each other. Savannah smiled and said with a slight hint of embarrassment, "Please be patient. I remember Ted and Jim talking about you and they speak very highly of you. I am sure I feel the same way, I just can't remember at the moment." It was interesting that she didn't quite remember Bob even though he was from her past and that block of memories seemed to be more intact.

While they were eating lunch, Savannah would look at Bob and on occasion a distant memory would flash through her mind. She was starting to remember him and as they talked about the old company, the fog in her head from that timeframe began to clear. She gave Bob a big smile at the thought of all those happy memories. Lunch was great and when they finally left the restaurant, Savannah gave Bob a hug saying that she was glad he was in her life. He smiled and told her to keep in touch.

It was the day before Savannah was going to leave and Trish felt she had done well in helping Savannah remember. She was putting pieces together here and there and remembering more every day.

Trish decided to take Savannah to her mother's grave. *Although it may be hard for her,* she thought, *it could open up another block of memories, which is a good thing.* With that she drove across town. As they passed a park, Savannah yelled out "Wait! I remember this park. My mom used to take me here all the time. We spent so much time swinging on the swings and sliding on the slide. Once, my mom even got me an ice cream from the ice cream man."

Savannah's face was beaming as she remembered, "It was a Neapolitan ice cream sandwich." Then she turned to Trish and exclaimed, "I remember!"

Trish was elated. She was still driving and wondering now if she should still make the trip to the cemetery. On a whim she said, "Savannah do you want to go visit your mother's grave? We can stop and get flowers and bring them to her."

Savannah looked over at her friend and Trish could almost see the memories unlocking in a methodical fashion.

"That's right." Her voice was a whisper. "Mom died. I remember now. It was one of the saddest days of my life. Yes, I would love to bring her flowers."

They stopped at a little stand just inside the cemetery and bought a bouquet of daisies. Savannah remembered instantly that they were her mom's favorite. When she saw the simple marker that told the story of her mother, tears started to stream down her face.

"Eileen Jacobs"

"My Mother"

"My Hero"

She looked up at Trish who had stepped back to allow her friend some alone time.

"I remember her," she said. She got up and hugged Trish. "Thank you for bringing me here."

They left the cemetery and headed to their favorite coffee shop. Savannah talked about what she was remembering about her mom and Trish filled in wherever she could, as necessary.

It was late when they got back to Trish's house. Bill looked up from where he was sitting. He was on the phone and when they opened the door they heard Bill say, "Oh here they are now. Savannah, it's Jim and he wants to talk to you."

Savannah took the phone and talked to Jim. She told him everything that she had done and how the memories had come back about her mother. She told him that she missed him and wanted to see him. And she wanted to see Sammy! Jim was so excited. *She* had mentioned Sammy first. He asked if she wanted to talk to him and she said, "*YES!*" Then she and Sammy talked on the phone. They talked about what he was doing and she told him she was coming home soon. Sammy was very happy and when Savannah got off the phone her smile was radiant. She looked at Trish and stopped short.

"What's the matter Trish?"

Trish looked at her friend and Savannah noticed her hand travel to the place where her unborn baby was lying in wait. Then they both looked down. Trish's water had broken and she stood there for a minute unsure of what had just happened.

"Your water broke Trish. The baby is coming soon." Savannah spoke with self-knowledge and Bill jumped to his feet and looked at Trish.

"Right now?" he asked in a panic. "Is it time to call the doctor?" Trish nodded and Savannah handed Bill's phone back to him as she still had it in her hand after hanging up with Jim.

Bill called the doctor and was told to wait a couple of hours and if she didn't go in to labor on her own they were going to induce labor. It was 5:30 p.m. and the doctor wanted her at the hospital no later than 8:00 p.m. Bill and Savannah rushed around making sure Trish's hospital suitcase was adequately packed, the infant car seat was in the car and a "go home" outfit for both a boy and a girl baby were neatly folded and included in Trish's suitcase. Trish was anxious but, at age 34, she was still in tiptop shape and was hopeful that labor would be smooth. All preliminary screenings had shown that the baby was healthy with no hint of any problems due to her age as a first-time mother.

At about 7:45 p.m. they decided it was time to head to the hospital. They all had a feeling that it was going to be a long night but they were ready and adrenaline was high. Trish took one more look at the beautifully decorated nursery and smiled knowing that soon her baby would occupy the room. She couldn't wait. With a smile on her face and excitement in her heart, they set off for the hospital.

It was a warm night in spite of being fall and the hospital parking lot was full. Trish said she was ok with parking further and walking, saying the walk would do her good. She had been sitting for a couple of hours now and her body ached to get up and stretch. As they started their walk however, Trish noticed a little spasm in her belly. She thought, *I won't say anything unless it gets worse.* Minutes later it did get worse and it was becoming harder and harder to walk. They were about halfway through the parking lot and Trish had officially gone in to labor.

"Guys" she said as she stopped walking and put her hands on her belly. "I think I am in labor. The walking must have started it."

With that, Bill directed Savannah to stay with Trish and he took off running to get a wheelchair. He was back in what seemed like seconds and within minutes he had wheeled her through the double doors to the emergency room. Trish was whisked away with Bill right by her side. Just before she went in to the delivery room however, Trish had the nurse stop. She looked at Savannah who had been standing there watching her friend get wheeled towards the double doors to the delivery room and vaguely remembering her own experience.

"I want Savannah to come in with us." Trish said it louder than she needed to as another intense pain riddled through her body. She looked at Savannah who was giving her a quizzical look. "It will help you to remember." She gasped as another spasm rippled through her belly. She smiled a labored smile.

The nurse shouted, "Hurry!" She had been mentally counting the time between contractions and knew they were less than two minutes apart.

They barely got everyone in the room and poised for delivery before Macie entered the world. She was beautiful and the second she announced her arrival, Savannah had tears streaming down her face. She looked at Trish as if to tell her that she remembered having a baby too. Savannah hugged Trish and told her how absolutely beautiful her baby girl was. Then she left the room to sit outside and think. Savannah remembered now the delivery of her own child but her memory seemed to fail her of his life up until now. She was empty and although she dug down as deep as she could, she couldn't remember. She thought about the loving gesture that Trish had shown her by allowing her to be in the delivery room at such a special moment. She realized what a wonderful friend she had in Trish.

She looked at the pictures of Sammy on her phone and closed her eyes but couldn't piece together the time in her life from Sammy's birth until the accident. She called Jim and told him the news of the baby. She also told him she had remembered giving birth to Sammy but then her memory stopped. She started to cry right there in the empty waiting room and it broke Jim's heart.

"You will remember Savannah. It will just take time. When you get home we can start making new memories, as your little boy is anxious to see you! He drew a picture of you reading him a story. He remembers and he will help you."

Jim's words comforted her and she hung up the phone feeling hopeful. His words about Sammy gave her motivation. Her brave little boy was trying to help *her*.

When Bill came out of the room it was very late. They didn't want visitors until morning and Savannah's plane left at 1:30 p.m. Bill took Savannah home to get some sleep. He promised to drive her back to the hospital to see Trish and the baby before she had to leave in the morning.

They talked all the way home about how beautiful little Macie was and how quickly she had come into the world. Trish was doing great but she was definitely tired. Bill was going back to the hospital to sleep with Trish and the baby. He said he would come back for Savannah in the morning to take her first back to the hospital then to the airport. Savannah asked if they could stop by the mall in the morning. She wanted to buy something nice for Trish and the baby. Bill was up for that, as he wanted to get his daughter something special too.

Morning came quickly and after she had toast and coffee, Bill arrived. It was early and the mall had just opened. Bill bought Macie an adorable outfit that said "Daddy's girl." It was pink and white and had a picture of a ballerina on the front. It had some lace on the bottom of the long sleeves and around the ankles of the footed bottoms. It was darling.

Savannah looked all around until she saw the perfect gift. It was a statue of a mother angel holding her baby in her arms. It was just what she had been looking for and she couldn't wait to give it to Trish.

When they walked in the room Trish had her back to the door. She was dressed and sitting in the rocking chair looking down. When they walked around, they saw Macie in a nice soft yellow nightgown. She looked warm and happy as she nestled snuggly next to her mother. She had just finished nursing and was sound asleep. Trish looked radiant. You would have thought that she was the very first mother to have ever given birth. She looked so proud holding her baby. Savannah smiled and then her smile widened as the memories of those same feelings rushed into her head. The missing pieces seemed just out of reach and it was driving her crazy.

She gave Trish the angel and Trish cried and cried. "My hormones are crazy right now," she said "I cry over everything."

Just then Bill said, "Savannah we have to go or you will miss your flight."

Bill took the sleeping baby from Trish and she stood up to hug Savannah. They hugged a long time.

"Thank you – for everything," Savannah said to Trish. "You have opened up my world and made things so much clearer for me. I am close. I know I am. You, Bill and Macie come to California this summer. Promise?"

Trish smiled through teary eyes. "We will do our best. I love you Savannah."

"I love you too Trish" Savannah whispered.

And with that, she had to leave.

Jim and Sammy were scheduled to pick Savannah up at the airport. Halfway through her stay with Trish, Savannah had told Jim that she would be ok to fly home by herself and she thought that Jim should stay with Sammy.

"I want you both to come to the airport to pick me up," she had told Jim. Now she couldn't wait to see both of them. As the plane took off, she closed her eyes to think. She had that crazy dream again last night. The doctor had said it was from her past, but Trish had driven her all around town and nothing jogged her memory. She thought about all the things she knew that occurred. Going fast – running? Dark, she thought it was a tunnel, but now she was second guessing herself. Comforting eyes translated into a familiar face but she still couldn't figure out who it was.

CHAPTER
FORTY-TWO

"Mommy, Mommy!"

Sammy came running up and threw his arms around Savannah. This time she knelt down and hugged him back tightly. She thought, *I might not remember the first part of his life but I can remember him now.*

Jim hugged her and kissed her softly. She felt so good in his arms and he was happy to see her. On the way home he told her that he had invited Ted and Bette over for dinner. Ted had been asking how she was doing. When Bette heard that she was just getting home she insisted that they have dinner at their house.

Ted and Bette's house was comforting and they sat and listened while Savannah described her visit with Trish and Bill. When Bette called everyone to the table Ted said, "I would like to propose a toast."

Everyone was seated and raised their glasses to get ready for the toast. Even Sammy raised his little cup with a big smile on his face. Just then, they heard the familiar faint whistle of the train that went breezing through town the same time every evening.

Without thinking, Savannah looked at Sammy and said, "What's that?"

He looked at her with those beautiful eyes and smiled. Those eyes! Now she knew whom they had belonged to all those months in her dreams. They were Sammy's and the tunnel was from the train ride they had taken on his birthday not so long ago.

She jumped up and grabbed Sammy and hugged him close. To everyone else she whispered through happy tears, "I remember."

Savannah was home at last.

www.ingramcontent.com/pod-product-compliance
Lightning Source LLC
Chambersburg PA
CBHW070549180626
46817CB00005B/1753